RIDING
PLANET EARTH

Enjoy the ride!

Shelly C. Seidahl

More Junior Fiction by Roussan For you to enjoy

RIDING
PLANET EARTH

Shelley A. Leedahl

Cover illustration by Dean Bloomfield

ROUSSAN
PUBLISHERS INC.
Specializing in YA and fiction for pre-teens

THE CANADA COUNCIL | LE CONSEIL DES ARTS
FOR THE ARTS | DU CANADA
SINCE 1957 | DEPUIS 1957

We acknowledge the support of the Canada Council for the
Arts for our publishing program.

http://www.magnet.ca/roussan

Copyright © Shelley A. Leedahl

National Library of Canada

Bibiliotèque nationale du Québec

Canadian Cataloguing in Publication Data
Leedahl, Shelley A. (Shelley Ann), 1963-
Riding planet earth
ISBN 1-896184-26-X
I. Title.
PS8573.E3536R53 1997   jC813'.54   C97-900825-5
PZ7.L51523Ri 1997

Cover illustration by Dean Bloomfield
Cover design by Dan Clark
Interior design by Jean Shepherd

Published simultaneously in Canada and the United States

Printed in Canada

1 2 3 4 5 6 7 8 9 MRQ 02 01 00 99 98 97

This book is for Logan and Taylor.

Acknowledgement: The author would like to thank Don Crawford and his 1995/1996 Grade 6/7 class at North Park Wilson School in Saskatoon for their numerous suggestions and abundant support.

Prologue

By the end of the year it was clear that West Park School was not big enough for the both of us. In fact, all of Saskatoon may have been too small. We'd barely managed to survive the last half of grade seven together; grade eight was out of the question. One of us would have to go, and after all I'd been through…well, let's just say it was *not* going to be me.

Man, life should come with a warning label.

Chapter One

RINGO

It looked like an ancient fortress. Like something built to keep people out, or trap them inside. That's the first thing I thought when I saw the massive brick building. West Park School. My new home-away-from-home. "Nineteen twenty-two," Dad announced, jarring me back to the present century. He pointed to the plaque above the double doors. "That's almost as old as me!"

"Right, Dad." He's always cracking jokes, or trying to. Most of them flop, but at least he isn't one of those idiots who laugh at their own attempts. Anyway, he's blood, so sometimes I humor him. "You look pretty good for a guy in his mid-seventies."

He jogged up the dozen stairs to West Park's wooden doors, leaving me lonely on the sidewalk below. For the last two nights I'd been dreaming about what might lie behind those doors, because I knew that once I crossed the threshold, anything could happen.

"What are you waiting for?" Dad called.

He obviously didn't get it. It was bad enough being twelve and having to suffer through zits and those ultra-embarrassing birds and bees talks, but to be twelve, stuck with the name Ringo *and* starting at a new school in a new city in a new province in the middle of the year had to be the worst. There's just no justice on planet earth.

I trudged up the steps with what felt like lead bricks in my hiking boots, then locked my eyes on the door handle as if it were the enemy. Dad grabbed it. The jaws of the door opened wide.

"What were you expecting?" Dad asked. "Dragons?"

How'd he guess?

Just one step and I'd be in. The little voice in my head with the distinct English accent cheered me on.

Go on, Ringo, you can do it. Just one small step for mankind, or humankind, rather.

Then Dad pushed, and I was in.

We began walking down a hall as wide as a highway and my stomach did a back flip. Just wait till they get ahold of my name, I thought. We're talking major humiliation.

The name was Mom's bright idea. My parents are *still* crazy about the Beatles, even though the Fab Four split up centuries before I arrived on the scene. Mom's fave was, and is, Ringo Starr. It's John Lennon all the way for Dad. He burns a candle each year on the anniversary of Lennon's death. Kinda creepy, but who knows...maybe I'll burn a candle for someone when I'm old, too.

The school hallway seemed to go on forever, like it was the Trans-Canada of hallways or something. I checked behind me and sure enough, my boots had left a brown, watery trail across the shiny floor. Too late to do anything about it; we were at the office.

"Excuse me," Dad began, easily resting his elbows on the high counter top.

The secretary did a little pirouette and faced us. Her eyelids, heavy with purple powder and chunky black mascara, opened like drawbridges, wide but slow, as if they could barely support the make-up's weight. "Oh!" she popped, making her mouth an O. Her round, rouged cheeks turned an even deeper shade of red. They looked like two planets. Like Mars.

I notice things like make-up, probably because my mom is of the no-make-up mentality and no matter how determined you are *not* to be like your parents, some things are like chalk—bound to rub off.

I also notice people's first impressions of my dad. Starting from the top, he has a stubborn cowlick that makes him look like he's just rolled out of bed no matter how often he gels it down. A pretty normal looking face, with a scar sliced through one eyebrow where he took a slapstick when he was a Pee Wee. Acceptable hazel eyes, nose a little on the large side, and a mouth that often curves into a smile. His ears are okay, but he's started growing hairs out of them and this drives him wild. His most striking feature is his height, a full 6' 4". He says he didn't even start growing until he was eighteen, so there's hope for me yet, unless I get Mom's genes on this one. She's only 5'4". She stood on a box in their wedding picture.

Dad may look like a tough guy with that height and broad shoulders to boot, but he sure doesn't act like one. We're talking *real* mellow. I've known guys who were tigers and others who were snakes, but if my dad were an animal, he'd be a moose. I can easily picture him against a forest backdrop, standing in water up to his knobby knees, calmly munching on weeds. My mom would be something quick and sharp. A fox, maybe, or a jack rabbit. My sister would be a Tasmanian devil. I might be a common cocker spaniel: basically obedient, relatively smart, easily overlooked.

But back to Dad. His hands are as big as baseball gloves. People say that he'd been a pretty decent quarterback in high school and he still keeps himself in prime shape by running as often as he can. Well, to see him do it, it looks more like loping. Like anteloping.

He even lopes marathons a couple times a year. Anyway, as far as dads go, I could have done worse.

"I'm Jim Warren and this is my son Ringo," he boomed at the secretary. His voice matches his stature, kind of like a double whammy when you first meet him. "We've just moved to Saskatoon from Gibsons, British Columbia."

He paused, as if waiting for her to comment, but she didn't bat even one of those gobbed-eyelashes over my goofy name or our hometown, Gibsons, of *The Beachcombers* fame. Dad thinks the whole world should remember the TV show, just because it was Canadian and it aired for something like a thousand years.

"Ringo's in grade seven," Dad continued, in his one-way conversation.

The secretary grinned. She had pink lipstick smeared on her front tooth and I couldn't help staring. "Nice to meet you both," she said, extending a hand with long, lethal fingernails to have it lost in my father's. "Welcome." She opened the filing cabinet and passed Dad a form. Then with a twirl of a skirt that hugged her bottom she was off, knocking on a door at the back of the office. "Mrs. Krause, we have a new student."

I swallowed hard and steadied myself. The secretary swayed back toward us and nailed me with her eyes. "Have a seat," she invited, "it'll just be a minute."

My body settled into an orange plastic chair but my

head was about to fly off. I was wishing I'd brought a paper bag to breathe into before I hyperventilated.

This was always happening to me. Fear rose from my chest like a huge metal ball and lodged itself in my throat. Maybe that's where the expression *hard to swallow* comes from. I'm improving, but back then I found many things in life hard to swallow. Home, school, and just about everything in-between. Stress is my middle name. I'm sure I'll have gray hair before my parents do. Like next year, maybe. That should be a *real* turn-on for the high school girls.

I tried swallowing my fear again and concentrated on breathing slowly and deeply. Strange city, strange school; I felt like an alien.

Okay, chap. You haven't got time for all this bother. You've got to relax.

It was that annoying British dude in my head again. Ever since I can remember he's been telling me how to live my life. As if that's not enough torture, he often has company. Get this…it's the Beatles! Right then they broke into their hit ballad, *Let It Be*. A private concert inside my head. I've never told anyone, but in *my* times of trouble, their music often comes without warning and strangely enough, it sometimes helps.

I picked a thread off my new jeans and wondered why I'd worn the stupid things in the first place. Dad had hemmed them and turned them into flood pants. Plus, he was out of blue thread and had to use yellow.

The stitches practically glowed! My knapsack looked like it'd been through fifteen world wars, and wouldn't you know I was also having a bad hair day. It popped up like horns on each side of my head. Sheesh.

Breathe two three four. Breathe two three four. Come together now lad...you've got to get a grip. Look at the pros, not just the cons.

Okay, I agreed. Here goes.

Pros: no one knew about my weird family yet. My mother, who once chained herself to a tree in a logging protest and had to spend the night in jail; my sister, Jane, who was fifteen and living in a group home in Vancouver because she and her gang had burnt down a house; my dad, who saw himself as a cross between some super jock and a five star stand-up comic. More pros: my buddy Jeff had spent a few weeks in Saskatoon with his cousins and said there were tons of cute girls here. Well, he didn't actually say "cute girls," he said "hot chicks," but that's Jeff. Not exactly the most politically correct guy I know, but then he doesn't live with my mother. You'd think she worked for the word police.

As I saw it, the biggest con was not knowing anyone. This was especially bad because by grade seven everyone except the complete freaks probably had enough friends already. Anyone normal wouldn't want anyone new. It might upset the balance, disturb the rhythm. If West Park was anything like my old school, you wouldn't fit in unless you were a jock or a joker or incredibly lucky, and I struck out on all three. At least there I'd had Jeff, who was also a triple loser.

I tallied my cons. Con: eventually people might find out about my family. Con: we had to rent because our house in Gibsons hadn't sold yet. Our crammed apartment was a major drag. But the most pressing con was the one I was sure I was about to face any minute. That would come after the principal led me down the long shiny hall, rapped on a door and spoke briefly to some geeky teacher. The teacher would invite me in and I'd have to stand in front of the entire, gawking class. They might as well just hang a sign around my neck that said OPEN SEASON ON THE NEW GUY. TARGET PRACTICE BEGINS NOW.

But even that wouldn't be the worst. The worst would come after the teacher said something like, "Class, this is Ringo." *Snicker snicker.* "He's from British Columbia. Let's all say hello and extend a big West Park welcome," and then there would be a deafening silence. A silence so big you could drive around in it. You could get lost in it. That was the one that would get me.

Chapter Two

CRUSHED

My prediction was only half wrong; Ms. Harmon was the most ungeeky teacher a guy could wish for. First of all, she didn't seem old enough to be a teacher. She looked and dressed like somebody's teenage sister. Not mine, of course, but somebody's. Her hair was the color of pine cones. It was long, straight, luxurious hair that she either pulled back into a ponytail or left alone to swish and shimmer with every move she made.

I soon realized that I wasn't alone in watching every move she made. In fact, most of my male classmates seemed to hang onto her every word, as if her words were fish hooks and the guys were hungry fish. A neat trick, especially when you're a teacher.

She was just right in the make-up department—not so much that you'd know she was wearing it—and she had the greatest laugh, kind of loud, like she really meant it. She laughed a lot, and when she did her amazing eyes, eyes that matched her hair, sparkled, and sometimes I'd catch her blink away a tear. Then my stomach did another kind of flip flop.

Yep, I already had a crush. Big time.

Aside from Ms. Harmon, no one stood in line to make me feel welcome those first few weeks, but that's pretty much what I expected. New kids are usually treated like some strange breed that needs to be sniffed out and okayed before anyone gets too close. I know. I sniffed out a few myself back in Gibsons.

How's a guy supposed to act? I wondered. Should you pretend to like everyone you meet? Should you stay low-key, cross your fingers and hope you'll camouflage into the scenery?

My mom always says "Just be yourself," so that's who I was. Myself. Allow me to introduce you. Day one. Basketball. The real Ringo tripped over his own feet when he tried doing a lay-up. With everyone razzing me, I hardly even noticed the floor burns. When I finally got the moves down, I scored the winning basket. Terrific, right? Wrong. I got my directions screwed up and tossed the ball into the wrong net! I was so freaked I almost tossed my cookies, too.

So much for first impressions.

Then there was school work. We were having what Ms. Harmon called an old-fashioned spelling bee, guys against the girls, week two. Now I'm no brain or anything, no future rocket scientist, but I don't tend to have much trouble with spelling. Math problems make me crazy; sounding out words I can do.

So we were taking turns spelling these words and frankly, most of the guys were dropping like flies. The girls started feeling all superior, of course, and the stakes were high. The losers each had to write a 750 word essay on a Canadian author. Ms. Harmon, I learned, was hot for CanLit.

This Matt kid screwed up on *caliber*. And then it was my turn. I rattled off *anthology* and *marginal* and knocked out two opponents. The guys cheered, and I was starting to feel like maybe I'd fit in after all. Then a real looker went up to bat against me; a girl with a name just about as weird as my own.

Summer could have been a model, easy. She was my height, had shoulder-length, bouncy, golden hair and jade green eyes with black lashes that showed them off. When she smiled or laughed she revealed perfect teeth, and I wondered if she was blessed with them or'd had to endure braces. She must have played an angel in every Christmas play—she appeared born for the part—yet in her navy turtleneck and blue jean overalls she was also earthy, like someone who

18

wouldn't be afraid to get her hands dirty in the garden and wouldn't scream if she dug up a worm. Her lips were shiny. Lip gloss? I wondered what flavor.

Watermelon...strawberry...peach...bubble gum...

"Ringo!"

"Huh?" I'd been daydreaming, and it was my turn.

Ms. Harmon seemed to be stifling a smile, like she knew. "Your word is *choir*."

"Choir?" I had to make sure.

"That's right."

I scratched my head. "Like a group of people singing?"

Ms. Harmon probably thought I was trying to be a wise guy, but she answered without sounding annoyed. "That's generally what a choir is."

Somebody cawed.

"Aw, so easy," one girl whined.

"Pathetic," agreed another classmate. "That's a giveaway."

"Ringo?" Ms. Harmon tilted her head and a waterfall of hair fell over one shoulder. "Go ahead."

Suddenly everybody shut up. You could've heard a pin drop from Mount Everest. The guys had that desperate look in their eyes, as if to say *screw this up and you'll be writing fourteen essays on Canadian authors!*

Choir. My mind went as blank as fresh snow in a front yard, before any dogs or kids get into it. It was one of those trick words you couldn't sound out. I searched my brain files but couldn't remember if it started with a k or a qu or what.

"The clock's ticking, Ringo," Ms. Harmon reminded. Sweat blossomed above my upper lip and I felt a tingling sensation in my armpits. Sometimes deodorant just doesn't cut it, no matter what they say on TV.

My pretty opponent was smiling like a cat in the sun.

"Time's up, Ringo. Summer...can you spell choir?"

"No problem," she said, and proceeded to whip off the five correct letters.

"The girls win!" Ms. Harmon announced.

"Girls rule!" Tori, the class loudmouth, yelled. "Three cheers for the losers."

I wanted to melt into the floor.

"Boys, there are lots of books in the library by and about Canadian authors," Ms. Harmon said. "You can check them out over recess. And don't forget we have a number of excellent writers living right here in Saskatchewan. Have fun!"

I made a beeline back to my desk, head toward China. Larry, the class gorilla, who just happened to sit behind me, grunted in my ear for the rest of the day.

I was beginning to give up hope of ever having a social life again, or even of having one friend to call my own. Apart from my cheerless hours at school, my life pretty much revolved around the TV—soap opera after game show after sitcom, every day. I had most of the commercials memorized. *Never let them see you sweat*... dream on!

I was so bored I started to count the hairs on my head. I penned a face on each square of a toilet paper roll, then rolled it back up. I even helped Mom stuff envelopes for one of her save-the-something-or-other causes.

Then, when I was least expecting it, it happened. Somebody actually spoke to me at school! Well, I guess he kind of had to because Ms. Harmon paired us for a social studies project, but pretty soon after it was clear we were going to be buds.

Physically, Adam Harrison is a lot like me. Middle-of-the-road looks, a little under average in the height department. I thought he might be the type of kid who still thrived on making model airplanes and hung them from his bedroom ceiling, because his clothes were kind of on the lame side—button up shirts, ironed jeans and a belted winter coat that made him look like an English schoolboy. I was surprised to learn that this sandy-haired kid with the chipped front tooth was actually a pretty cool guy.

Adam has this easygoing personality that makes other people feel comfortable. There were always lots of girls around his desk, but I got the sense that they were pals, not potential dates. He didn't think he was God's gift to women, like Matt Webster, who was also in the popular crowd, and Adam wasn't a brown-noser, like Bobby Cameron, whom everyone called Bobby Brown-Noser or just Bobby B., for short. That loser sucked up to everyone! It was Adam who gave me my first lesson in Larry.

We were on a school skating excursion at an outdoor rink. We'd had a hat trick of horrible weather since I'd arrived but this bunch seemed not to mind. It was like their skin was thicker, hardier. Personally, I would have preferred another hour of hard time in French class rather than venturing out and losing an ear or nose to frostbite.

I'd only been in Saskatoon twenty-some days, but I was starting to wonder if this part of Canada would ever warm up. Even though the sky was a summer blue and the sun was still perched up there in its usual spot, it didn't make any difference. The cold clung to me like a second, brittle skin. In Gibsons it never got very cold, so I was bitter. Bitter *and* brittle as thin ice.

Anyway, this was no ordinary rink, which kinda made up for the cold. It was right downtown beside the river and this serious hotel called the Delta Bessborough. And I thought the school looked like a castle. This place had turrets and medieval-looking windows and it seemed to go up and up forever. I half expected Rapunzel to throw her long hair out of one of the windows.

Adam saw me gawking. "Earth to Ringo. Anybody home?"

"Huh?" I gave my head a shake.

My friend pointed to the hotel. "Everyone calls it The Bez. Pretty cool, eh?"

I was dizzy from looking up for so long and had almost forgotten why we were there.

"Time to slap these babies on," Adam reminded me. I'd slung my skates over my shoulder and he gave them a tug.

As we laced into our skates and the first few keeners hit the ice, a minor detail crept through my mind: I'm not the best skater in the world. For the next hour or so, I more or less fluked my way across the rink with my shins burning and my weak ankles splayed like Charlie Chaplin's. Adam didn't seem to notice, maybe because he was more concerned with dodging a fast-flying puck than worrying about my form. He ducked out of the way once more, just in time.

"That guy's a complete jerk," Adam declared, jutting his chin toward the big kid in the lumber jacket who was slapping a puck across the ice and nailing whoever he could. It was Larry. No one else had brought a stick.

"He doesn't say much in class," I said, giving Larry the benefit of the doubt. "Grunts quite a bit, but doesn't say much."

"It's just been a slow month for him," Adam assured me. He turned so that he was skating backwards and facing me. "Just wait."

I didn't have to wait long, because just then Larry skated up behind Adam and reefed on his back so hard my friend slammed into me. Wham! We bodychecked the ice. My arm was crushed beneath me, but I shook it out and didn't let on.

"What was that for?" Adam asked, brushing snow off his jeans as he stood.

"Because I felt like it," Larry barked, leaning on his hockey stick, elbow out.

He had that sheepdog look that parents love to hate: ratty bangs that hung way past his eyes, eyes which slid from Adam to me.

"And I didn't appreciate having to write an essay because of your lack of brains!"

"That was weeks ago!" Adam said in my defense.

Larry ignored him and poked me in the forehead with his ungloved pointer finger. "You screwed up, little girl. Whatcha gonna do about it?"

He kept jabbing my forehead and I slowly slid backwards on my skates. I felt like grabbing his finger and biting, but then he'd have said I fight like a girl, too.

"Ringo," he mocked, his top lip curled in a sneer, "you sure it's not Bingo?" His laugh was like a scrape. "Nice name...for a dog."

Other skaters were gathering to see what would happen next. I waited for them to start chanting *fight fight*, but then Ms. Harmon and Mr. Crawford, the vice-principal, caught wind of the commotion and began skating our way.

Larry spit on my skates, then sped off, spraying snow at a group of girls when he stopped sharp, just inches behind them.

"Loser!" Adam called after him, but not loudly enough for Larry to hear.

"What's going on here?" Mr. Crawford asked, but no one offered any hints and the crowd split like pool balls in every direction. "Okay everyone, skates off and let's get back on the bus," he continued. Frost clung to his mustache and eyebrows. "And Larry," he called, "give me that blessed stick! If you can't behave we won't have any more field trips."

He and Ms. Harmon began gliding toward the toasty-warm shelter where we'd left our boots. My teacher's long hair sailed behind her.

Bobby B. whipped past us like his pants were on fire. "Do you need help with anything, Ms. Harmon? Can I sit with you on the bus? Can I? Huh? Can I?"

I grabbed a handful of snow to wipe the gob off my skates. It was already starting to freeze.

"Adam! Ringo!"

I turned to the voice of my spelling bee opponent, Summer. Had she been waiting for us? I didn't want to get my hopes up. Summer was a knockout and I was just...well...me. She looked like a carnival queen in her matching red headband, scarf and mittens. I'd noticed she skated like one, too. Many tried the one-foot-spin, but few could pull it off.

She glided toward us. Unlike me, she didn't look like she was about to crack in half from the cold. I hoped I didn't have any snot on my face, and did a quick swipe with my glove, just in case.

"I suppose Adam's already warned you about Larry," Summer began, stopping inches away from me.

I kept my head bowed, as if the ice held great interest. Summer's skates looked new. "Yep, he warned me."

I didn't know what else to say. Sometimes my tongue gets twisted up like a pretzel when I'm around pretty girls. They usually bolt after they discover what a dweeb I am, but to my amazement, Summer was hanging in there. I was afraid that if I looked directly at her she might skate away or simply disappear in a puff of smoke, but I took the chance. She pushed some hair away from her eyes. The wind blew it right back.

"Be careful," she said. "Larry's dangerous."

I thought she might be overreacting, but then Adam nudged me and pointed to his chipped tooth. "See this? This is some of Larry's handiwork."

I must have been standing there with my mouth hanging open, because Adam patted me on the back and said, "Don't worry, buddy. There's strength in numbers."

Then Summer touched the sleeve of my coat and

smiled right at me. Suddenly I knew why her parents had named her that. When she smiled I forgot about the outrageous temperature and the icy windchill. I forgot that the class bully was more than capable of physical violence and that Mr. Crawford was suggesting that we get our butts in gear. *NOW!*

Aside from Summer's smile and how it warmed me inside and out, all I could think of was how I'd have to write Jeff back in Gibsons and tell him he was right: there really were some hot chicks in cold Saskatoon.

Chapter Three

THE HOME FRONT

I expected the worst after the rink incident but Larry left me alone for the rest of the afternoon. Well, kind of alone. If you don't count that he tripped me on the bus and then, when he was helping me up, stuck a Kotex pad on my jacket. I can't imagine where he got it from. Maybe he keeps a bunch of props up his sleeve so he's always ready to humiliate someone. Fortunately, Adam peeled it off before too many people saw. Before Summer saw.

Then I had to survive the classroom. I could feel Larry's hateful gaze aimed at the back of my head like lasers, and by the time the final bell rang I could've sworn I had two holes burned into my skull.

I never got a chance to drill Adam about the chipped tooth. After school he had to fly home because his family was going to visit friends in Regina over the weekend.

"I'll spill my guts on Monday," he promised, zipping his knapsack.

We bumped our way down the hall of charging students, everyone anxious for the two school-free days. It reminded me of that place in Spain where once a year they let bulls loose in the streets and people actually run with them. Of course some people get gored, but I suppose that's half the fun.

Once outside, Adam turned left and I hung a right. "Later!" I called after him.

Home was five blocks from school, which gave me lots of time to rattle the events of the day around in my head, like pinballs in a machine. Turns out, I wasn't alone in there.

Well then, what do you make of it?

Oh, it's you again, I thought, the mighty, invisible Englishman. What do I make of what?

Your mate, with the chipped tooth. I'd be very concerned about this Larry chap.

I automatically ran my tongue along my smooth teeth. I sure hoped Larry wasn't singling me out as his next victim. I kind of liked my teeth just the way they were.

He sounds like a bit of a rotter.

Don't get your crap in a knot, I said to the voice. You're not even real. Now, I'm trying to think here, so take a hike, boy scout! The voice didn't utter another cockney word, and soon I was back at the apartment.

"Hey!" I said, stomping my boots on the doormat.

"Hey yourself," Dad answered. He was peeling potatoes at the sink and listening to a Beatles CD. Always the comic, he'd tied an apron on over his sweat pants and wrapped a pink towel around his head. "What do you think?" he asked. "Is it me?" He did a little dance and began singing along to *Lady Madonna*.

"The apron's fine," I said, matter-of-factly, "but you've *got* to do something about those shoes." I dropped my gaze to his tattered size thirteen Nikes— his good luck shoes. He'd placed second in his age group in a Vancouver marathon in those shoes; he'd wear them until they literally fell off. Even then, he'd probably snap elastic bands around them to keep them together.

I tossed my math homework onto the coffee table, where it would likely sit until Sunday night, and plopped onto the couch. "Make lots of potatoes," I ordered. "I'm starved."

I closed my eyes and rubbed my aching shins. Soon I was floating in that bizarre yet comfortable place that comes just before sleep. When the CD finished playing the only sounds were the gurgling of the potatoes and the occasional thump from the apartment above us. It was hard to get used to other people's sounds. I heard every creak and crash and my imagination went wild with the possibilities. If I really concentrated, I could even hear our neighbors' bathroom noises. Kinda funny, until I realized they could hear mine, too. From then on I tried not to let anything rip.

I guess Dad was tangled up in his own thoughts. Being unemployed was a drag, he'd said. I knew he'd sent out a whack of resumes but hadn't had even one interview yet. No one gave him a chance. Mom tried explaining to me that unemployment wasn't always high in Canada, and she looked forward to a time when things would turn around. "Jobs for all," was one of her favorite rants when she started raving about politics. I tuned her out like a radio station with a bad signal.

I didn't mind so much that Dad wasn't working. It was kinda cool having him at home after school and it meant I was no longer one of those latchkey kids that shrinks love to dissect, but I knew we couldn't go on like that for much longer—money was tight. Dad needed a job and even though I hated the thought of anyone else living in *my* house in Gibsons—the house where I'd written a secret code in the wallpaper at the top of the stairs and planted a time capsule beneath the floorboards in the kitchen—I knew it absolutely had to sell. We were packed into our two-bedroom apartment like sardines in a can, and we'd had to put lots of our stuff in storage, including my beloved bike.

As much as Dad loves running, I love biking. Even if I couldn't ride in the winter, I liked to be able to admire my mountain bike, my blue beauty, every once in a while. Probably guys with horses feel the same way about them. They become part of you.

"Thinking about spring?" Dad asked, sneaking up on my thoughts.

"How'd you guess?" He seemed to have a knack for knowing where my head was at, which was usually okay, but there are also times when you definitely *don't* want your dad to creep into your fantasies.

"Call me psychic," he said.

"Psychic."

I opened my eyes. Dad was bent over the couch like a tree in the wind. Uh huh! He hadn't read my thoughts after all. I'd been doodling in my semi-conscious state and had created a rough sketch of a guy on a bike. A guy who looked a lot like me, with bone-straight brown hair and skinny legs and arms, on a blue bike much like mine. "Wow, that's not half bad!"

Water hissed and splashed onto the stove. "Everyone take cover! It's erupting!" Dad warned, arms pinwheeling as he zigzagged toward the stove.

I licked my lips, anticipating the mashed potatoes, leftover gravy, pork chops and peas. Then, without warning, I was thinking about Larry again. I hoped he wasn't like the pot of potatoes that had simmered for so long and then finally boiled over. Maybe it was a sign. What a way to ruin a guy's appetite.

"Is Mom coming home soon?" I asked, needing to be distracted.

"Any minute," Dad called from the kitchen.

I stretched my arms above my head and yawned. "So how does she like her new job?"

"Loves it," Dad answered. He began whistling *Love Me Do*, another Beatles classic.

Mom had been the reason for the move. Over the last few years she's become ultra-political and now everything is a campaign to her. I'm still not exactly sure what her new job is, but it has something to do with unions and negotiating and when she got it Dad said it was right up her alley.

In the course of my lifetime Dad's been a drywaller, a church caretaker and a taxi driver. Oh yeah. He'd also had a brief and miserable turn as an insurance salesman. Suits and ties, he said, were not his color. Unemployment wasn't his color either.

Mom didn't get too hung up on the fact that she was the only one bringing in any cash. Actually, I think she was proud to be supporting the family, even though it meant a no-frills lifestyle. "We're not frilly people, anyway," she said. I knew that when Dad did find something new it would be back to splitting bills and negotiating housework.

I heard a rattle at the door. "Hey, Ringo! How about a hand over here." Mom was juggling a briefcase and a lumpy bag of groceries. I took the groceries and headed for the kitchen.

"How was your day?" she asked after me.

"Fine."

"How fine is fine?"

Man—sometimes she was relentless. "About an eight on a scale of one to ten," I lied, but what was I going to say? The school bully's out to get me? A pretty girl talked to me and I could barely look her in the eye? Paul, John, George and Ringo won't shut up and there's also some other English guy roaming around in my head? I said nothing. Besides, I didn't want to give my parents anything more to worry about. My sister, Jane, still in Vancouver, gave them plenty enough.

Mom set her briefcase on the table, then took off her long coat and hung it in the crammed closet. "Eight out of ten is great. How was your day, Jim?"

Dad had shed the apron and tea towel and now looked more like what he really was: an unemployed, thirty-seven-year-old man draining potatoes in the kitchen sink. A man trying to make the best of a bad situation. "You know what they say...no news is good news."

"Maybe tomorrow," Mom tried. A cloud of concern swept across her face then just as quickly disappeared.

Dad didn't see. Mom detoured down the dim hall and into the first bedroom. When she returned she was wearing baggy sweats, just like Dad, and her best "we're going to get through this" look.

About the clothes—my parents really know how to grunge. I've heard that rich people dress up for supper; in our family, we dress down.

The air held a burnt smell. "Dinnah is served," Dad announced, in a bad English accent.

Great, I thought, now I'm getting it in stereo. He'd slung a tea towel over his arm like he was serving a ritzy meal, not potatoes and pork chops and yesterday's gravy.

We sat at the round table in our usual places. If Jane would have been there, she'd be sitting across from me, but that chair had been empty for over a month already, and it felt weird, like even though she wasn't there in person, her presence was still with us. A ghost. I think we all felt it.

Mom rubbed her hands together like a fly. "Everything looks so good, Jim." She pointed with her fork to the red stuff on the meat. "What did you put on the pork chops?"

Dad swallowed a mouthful of peas. "Chili powder."

Mom shot him a strange look, but she took two crisp pork chops all the same. Meanwhile, I was loading up on potatoes. When I'd heaped a huge pile onto my plate, I burrowed out the center and filled it with gravy. "Mmm, delicious," I crooned, cramming the creamy mixture into my mouth as if it were the last meal I'd ever have.

Mom shook her head. "I'll give you until you're thirteen to keep making those disgusting potato sculptures. Then you start eating like an adult."

"It's not a sculpture and I—"

The phone jangled on the wall and Mom, who's forever winning our races to answer it, beat me again.

"Hello? Of course I'll accept the charges." She cupped her hand over the receiver and whispered, "It's Jane."

Dad's eyes zeroed in on mine as I slid back into my chair.

"Jane! How are you...what? So soon?"

I tried to read Mom's face.

"I didn't mean it like that Jane, I just didn't think that...of course I want you here...this is our home now." Mom's knuckles were white as bone on the receiver. "But you're only fifteen!"

She was coming completely undone. Jane had that effect on all of us, but mostly on Mom. She'd lost the color in her cheeks and her eyes darted from Dad to me to the calendar on the wall, like an owl. She motioned to Dad and mouthed "help."

"But we're a family!" she continued. Her voice was like a siren, or maybe I was just hearing the sirens in my own head. Police, ambulance, fire, they were all there, bright lights flashing.

Dad grabbed the phone. "Jane, we miss you. You have to come home, Honey. We already went over this. Saskatoon's like a brand new start for all of—"

While Dad continued pleading with my sister, Mom paced back and forth across the yellow linoleum. "I should've known she'd pull something like this." Tears were glossing her eyes. "I never thought having a daughter would be this hard. She doesn't even like me."

"Of course she does, Mom. She loves you. Jane's just screwed up. It's those people she hangs around with." I wasn't just saying this to make Mom feel better, I believed it was true. The trouble all started when Jane began hanging with a rough crowd.

"Ringo," Mom said, pulling me close and stroking my hair as if I were still a little boy. "You've never given me any grief."

Basically obedient. That's me.

I was having trouble breathing with my nose and mouth mashed against Mom's neck, but I hung in there for as long as I could. "Mom?" My voice was muffled. "Can I finish my potatoes now?"

Moments later Dad hung up the phone and returned to our cold meal. "She's flying in from Vancouver next Friday."

Chapter Four

SQUEAK!

On Monday morning I cornered Adam by the lockers.

"So, what happened?" I was panting.

He shoved some books into his messy locker and slammed it shut before they fell out. "Huh?"

"The chipped tooth," I rasped, ticked off that he'd forgotten he was going to tell me. "You know," I leaned toward him, making sure no one was within earshot, "between you and Larry?"

"Oh, that! He nailed me last spring on the ball field. He was pitching—not a wise position for a maniac—and when I stepped up to bat—BAM! He creamed me. Of course he claimed it was an accident, but it wasn't. Just like Matt's bike disappearing wasn't an accident…Bobby B.'s broken collar bone…Summer's money going missing…Stephen's seven stitches—"

"Hold it! Larry was responsible for all that?"

"And more," Adam said, spinning his combination lock. "The thing is, he always manages to come up with some explanation. There's always an alibi. Doesn't hurt to have parents who are lawyers. It could come in handy when he starts committing the *really* big crimes."

"No way! *Both* his parents are lawyers?" I swallowed the bird in my throat and it went down, wings flapping.

"Yep. You should see his house! A universal gym, indoor pool, intercoms in every room."

I had no trouble picturing it, like a mansion you'd see in the movies, but something didn't jive. "How do you know? I thought you hated him. Why were you at his house?"

Adam bent to tie his shoelace. "I haven't been for a zillion years. When we were in grade one, and Larry was only beginning his criminal activities, like breaking my crayons, I went to his birthday party."

"And?"

"He threw me in his pool," Adam said, standing again. "The deep end. I couldn't swim."

"Geez." Those wings were still flapping in my gut.

The bell rang and we made it through the maze of students to our homeroom, where I found the desk behind mine empty. I hoped Larry was sick. Measles would be good. Or mumps. Even mononucleosis, the kissing disease. I've heard that can knock you out for a long time, but no, it wasn't possible. Who'd ever want to kiss Larry?

I peeked at Summer, two rows over, and to my surprise she was peeking at me, too. We both quickly turned away, but my heart filled like a balloon and I couldn't help smiling to myself. Was there hope that a goddess like her might actually be interested in a goof like me? She and Tori must have called each other because they were both wearing dresses and funky platform shoes. They looked wicked!

Matt, on my left, was combing his fingers through his long hair and checking it out in a hand-held mirror. It was gelled straight back, like an oil slick. A seagull would get stuck in it, easy. I could tell by the way he kept wiping his hands on his jeans that his whole head was a sticky mess.

Bobby Brown-Noser was straightening the chalk on the blackboard ledge when Ms. Harmon waltzed in. That kid really lived up to his name.

"Good morning, class," Ms. Harmon said in her singsong voice. She was looking especially awesome in a pair of cream-colored leggings and a matching sweater. Gold stars and silver moons shone from her earlobes. Artsy earrings. The kind you buy at street fairs. "As you know Valentine's Day is coming up and we'll be having a dance. It's free and—"

The door creaked open and Larry dragged his feet across the floor. "I missed the bus," he said, "and I couldn't get a ride."

When he threw himself into the desk behind me I felt my own desk lift off the floor.

"That's okay," Ms. Harmon replied, her voice soothing in the large classroom, as if it brought the walls closer together and made everything cosy. "As I was saying, we're having a Valentine's dance on Friday and I encourage you all to attend. And please...bring music from home."

I turned to Adam and we both raised our eyebrows. I liked dancing. I was even kinda good at it. Me, Mom and Dad were always dancing at home. Even Jane used to, before she thought that dancing and everything else our family did was uncool. But what about music? Aside from everything the Beatles ever produced, we didn't exactly have a great selection, and what if people thought I was bizarre? I mean, the Beatles were ancient! I'd skip the music thing, but I couldn't wait for that dance.

"Now let's pick up where we left off last class," Ms. Harmon continued. "You were to read chapters eight and nine."

I dug into my desk for the book but my fingers poked against something else. Fur? I dared to move my finger another inch. "Ahhh!"

Every head spun toward me.

"Ringo...what's wrong?" Ms. Harmon asked.

I gritted my teeth and pulled a very dead, very stiff white rat out of my desk by its long tail. "It's a...it's a..."

"It's a dead rat!" Summer screeched.

"Gross!"

"Ohhh!"

"Disgusting!"

I could have puked right there, but I managed to keep my eggs and toast in place. Larry, I noticed, didn't speak a single syllable.

"It looks like it's been in there all weekend," Ms. Harmon deduced. She held a bag at arms length and I plopped the rat in. She tied the end in three knots. "Who's responsible for this?" she demanded, holding the bag away from her body.

Everyone immediately clammed up and looked around the room like someone would confess. As if!

"Not only is this a despicable, unhealthy thing to do, but to think that someone may have actually killed this creature to torment a fellow student is...is...well it's appalling!" She dropped the bagged rat into another bag. "If anyone has any information on this matter, see me at recess. Ringo, please take this right outside to the dumpster, then wash your hands thoroughly with plenty of soap and the hottest water you can stand."

I did as I was told, trying to shake the image of the double-bagged rat. Dead weight. In two Safeway grocery bags.

The sky was spitting sticky, wet snow when I opened the door. The Beatles' song *Yesterday* sailed through my thoughts as I approached the bin. I was thinking about the irony of the song. It'd been a lot longer than yesterday since my troubles were far away. Sorry boys, I thought, wrong number this time.

In the bathroom I pumped a green pool of soap into my hands, then shot them under a blast of hot water, practically scalding myself.

I say, do be careful. You may be needing those.

Yeah, I said to my reflection in the mirror. For self-defense.

When me and my red hands returned, the class was into an enthusiastic discussion on the novel we were reading. All that chatter proved to be the perfect opportunity for Larry to poke me in the back with a pencil. A sharp pencil. *Lead poisoning,* I thought. Then I felt his hot breath on my ear.

"Squeak," he squeaked.

Only one little word, but it was enough.

Chapter Five

HAPPY VALENTINES

Why is it that when you're waiting for something time travels about as fast as a slug? That's how it was waiting for Friday, sluggish, but the day and the hour of the Valentine's dance finally arrived.

Summer, Tori and most of the other girls were wearing red, pink or purple for the special occasion. If I was the poetic sort I'd say they looked like a row of carnations, sitting across the gym on "the girl's side," but I'm not the poetic type. That's Summer's department. Turns out she has a real way with words, and she shared some of those words with the class through a poetry reading.

Summer writes confessional poems. We're not talking flowers and butterflies and cute little rhymes—these are real life poems about some of the crap she's had to suffer through, namely, her father's lies and her parents' separation and how those events shattered her world.

I'd sure never have the guts to spill personal stuff like that in front of the whole class, but obviously Summer did, and even Larry must have been spellbound, because he forgot all about poking me or breathing down my back. Some of the girls were crying when Summer finished. Man, just when I thought *my* life was rough. It kinda put things into perspective. At least for a few hours.

But back to the dance. Summer was a vision—a lavender turtleneck that would be soft to the touch; hair swept back from her slightly-flushed face; dangling heart-shaped earrings; faded jeans. She probably could have shown up in a bathrobe and hospital slippers and had me swooning, because it was always more than clothes and jewelry with that girl. She was comfortable in her own skin. She wore it well.

Tori, on the other hand, glared. From her blazing red jeans and candy-apple red T-shirt right down to her red-as-roses nail polish, she was like a walking, breathing stop sign.

The guys just didn't get into the Valentine's color theme in quite the same way. "What—no pink?"

Adam asked, looking me over as we took our place on "the boy's side" of the gym.

I pulled at the waist of my pants and pointed. "It's underneath."

"Really?" Adam leaned over as if to peek at my underwear, which actually was kinda pink because of one of Dad's famous laundry screw-ups: he mixed whites with a dark red towel.

I pushed Adam and smirked. "You'll never know."

Then: music. Mrs. Krause, the principal, turned off half the gym lights in an attempt to get people out on the dance floor. I was shy in front of Summer and her friends; total blackness would have been better yet. At first no one moved, then the music was cranked a few notches and a group of grade five girls got up and danced together in a circle. They were kinda stiff at first, but as soon as one brave soul tried something new it was like a chain reaction until pretty soon it looked more like a game of Simon Says than it did like dancing.

"It's a copycat dance," I said, nudging Adam who was smirking behind his hand. "Anything you can do I can do, too."

I started tapping my foot to the beat, but I knew how these things went. By the time I got up the nerve to ask anyone to dance the teacher would be calling out "last song." I wished confidence was something you could buy or borrow. If it was, maybe Matt would be willing to lend me some of his. A new song started and he asked Summer to dance, and Tori soon followed with a tall grade eighter who hopped from foot to foot like he was stepping on hot coals.

Adam elbowed me in the ribs. "Now or never, big guy." He grabbed my elbow and pulled me across the gym toward the girls. I didn't even know everyone's name yet, who was I going to ask?

"Ask Karen. She'll dance with anyone," he said, referring to a girl I'd seen hanging with Tori and Summer. Karen had just returned from a family vacation in South America where she claimed to have seen Brad Pitt on the beach. This alleged sighting had given her celebrity status, at least among the other girls. "I'll ask Bailey."

Karen saw us coming and probably knew Adam had put me up to it, but when I asked her to dance she said yes. We found a spot in the middle of the gym where people on the sidelines couldn't watch and crack jokes about us. Karen was about a head taller than me.

"You're a good dancer," she offered, loudly, so I could hear over the blaring music. I looked up. She'd sunburned her nose and the skin was flaking off.

"Who me?" I hadn't really been trying, just shuffling my feet and playing my air guitar.

Karen laughed. "Yes, you."

"Geez...thanks. You dance too good. I mean you

dance good, too." I was losing it. Thankfully, Karen changed the subject.

"They still haven't found out anything about that rat yet, hey?"

"Nope," I said, striking a chord in the air. "We probably never will." I had my own theory, of course. I thought Larry bought it at a pet shop, killed it—I don't know how, there was no autopsy—then stashed it in my desk Friday after class. I didn't dare accuse him without evidence, however, son of two lawyers that he was. I wondered why he wasn't at the dance, as it would be a great place to stir up some trouble. "Does everyone come to these things?"

Karen was really working it. "Usually," she said, huffing. A line of sweat had formed across her forehead, misting her thin bangs.

I glanced through the gyrating bodies to the side of the gym. "What about Larry?"

"No...he never comes to school dances. Thinks he's too cool."

"I've got a sister he should meet," I said, thinking out loud.

"What?" Karen cupped her hand around her ear.

"I said, I've got a blister on my feet." I saw no point in dragging out the family's dirty laundry. "On my heel. New shoes." I pointed. They didn't look new.

Karen just nodded. When the song was over I thanked her for the dance, then felt a tap on my shoulder. I turned to Summer's wide green eyes.

"Want to dance?" she asked. "I promise I won't ask you to spell anything."

"Spell anything?" I gave my head a shake.

Summer sunk her hands in her back pockets and leaned forward. "You know...the spelling bee?"

I must have been wearing a puzzled look, then memory came crashing back. "Oh yeah, you creamed me." We both smiled and the temperature rose about five degrees.

"Sorry about that," she said through her smile. "So...we dancing?"

"Sure!" I followed her to the middle of the floor, just as Mrs. Krause got on the microphone again like some deejay at a wedding dance. "And now we're going to slow things down a bit. Here's a waltz for all you valentines out there."

"Sorry," Summer apologized, "I didn't know."

"No problem," I said, my heart swelling.

Summer slid her arms around my neck. We were touching!

Breathe two three four. Breathe two three four. You can do this, Ringo.

Things were happening so fast! I managed to remember to wrap my arms around her waist, and we swayed to the music, each gazing past the other's ear. I was soon aware of the distance between us, and wondered what she'd think if I pulled her closer.

"I'm having a party in two weeks," she blurted. "It's my birthday. Can you come?"

"Sure!" I said. She was probably beginning to think I had a limited vocabulary. Adam was now dancing with Heather, one of the quieter girls in our class. He seemed to be bringing her out, because they were laughing and appeared to be having a really good time. "Is Adam going to your party?"

"Everyone," Summer said. "It's my mom's rule. I can't have a party unless I invite the whole class."

The *whole* class. It sounded like something *my* mom would make *me* do. That twisted ball of fear started to rise from my gut to my mouth and I was terrified it would come rolling out as a scream. I had to change the subject. "So how did you wind up with a name like 'Summer?'" I asked. Then, because I thought she might feel I was making fun of her, I added, "because I think it's a beautiful name."

"Do you really? Thanks! Well, my parents weren't exactly traditional about anything. In fact, when I was a baby, Dad stayed home with me and Mom continued working. But that was a long time ago." Her voice seemed to darken, as if sliding from sunny yellow to muddy brown. "Mom and I live alone now."

"Th-that's just like at our house," I said, tripping over the words.

"You live alone with your Mom, too?"

"No. Dad's with us...I meant the other part. My

50

dad's unemployed and Mom works full-time. That's why we moved here. She got a new job."

"No kidding!" So your dad, like, cleans and cooks and everything?"

Summer seemed genuinely interested, and I felt *her* arms pull *me* closer.

"Well, he really tries," I said, recalling some of his mystery meals.

"What about your name?" Summer asked, steering the conversation just as I steered us out of another couple's way.

"They called me Ringo after—"

"Ringo Starr," Summer spurted, completing my sentence.

I nodded. "You guessed it."

"I knew that had to be it." She threw her hair back and I caught a faint fragrance of flowers.

I was thrilled to learn she'd been thinking about me, even if it was just about how I got my dopey name. We danced closely until the song was over and Mrs. Krause split the air.

"Okay, now we're going to speed things up a little bit," she announced, and I could hardly believe what she said next: "Here's the Beatles doing *Twist and Shout.*"

"I love this song!" Summer squealed, jumping out of my arms. "Will you dance again? I think the Beatles are just the best!"

I guess you just never know.

We danced three more times before the lights were turned on and the dance ended. I had the feeling that people were gossiping about us. Let them talk! I thought. When Matt gave me a dirty look I just smiled and winked. What was it to him who I danced with?

"Thanks," Summer said, straightening a barrette that had slid down her silky hair. "That was a blast! Now I've got to pick up my CDs. See you back in class."

"Yeah. See you!" Suddenly this cocker spaniel was feeling more like a German shepherd, or a red setter, or a collie. One of those cocky dogs that struts down the street, proud of itself.

"Quite the Romeo, aren't you?" Matt snarled as he stepped up beside me in the hall. It looked like a seagull had in fact landed in his normally perfect hair. Landed and flapped its wings around.

"I'm sure I've got nothin' on you," I snapped.

"I'm sure you don't either!" He veered into the crowd, and Adam took his place.

"You've got lover-boy all jealous. He and Summer were going around together until about a month and a half ago."

"That's about when I came," I said, doing the math.

"You're catching on," Adam answered, cuffing me lightly in the back of the head.

We rounded the corner to find a noisy group gathered at the school's front entrance. "I wonder what's going on?" I said. It appeared that people were shoving each other to look out the windows in the double doors.

"Let's check it out," Adam advised and began butting his way through the curious mob. Tori, Bobby B., Heather and Matt were among the jostling students. Mr. Crawford was trying to herd everyone back to class.

"What a freak!" Matt yelled.

Tori looked like she'd just seen Frankenstein. "D-do you think she's coming in?"

"God, who'd want to do that to themselves?" Bobby B. wondered out loud.

I elbowed my way through the crowd, not thinking at all that this was Friday and what that meant besides the school dance.

"My God! She's completely bald!" Heather screeched.

I pushed Bobby B. out of my way and gawked outside. There, at the bottom of the steps, a teenager in black boots, torn jeans and a jean jacket with a long sweater hanging out the bottom was blowing smoke rings into the air, totally ignoring the faces in the window. She was cradling a book in one arm. My stomach cartwheeled and my knees gave out. MY book! I'd forgotten my science text and this rebel was my sister Jane, back from la-la land with a brand new look! How could she do this to me? Why did our parents let her come to the school? My head was exploding with questions.

Big breath in, big breath out. In…and out. That's it, Ringo. Nice and easy. You've come this far, don't want to blow it now.

"Who do you think that is?" Summer asked, wedging herself in beside me. "She's sure got guts."

I gave my sister one last look. She'd had green hair the last time I saw her, but even that was galaxies better than the shaved head. I felt all the blood drain from my face. How could I have forgotten she was coming home today?

"Ringo?" Summer was waiting. "Do you know who that is?"

I turned to her and, out of habit, crossed my fingers behind my back. "Haven't got a clue."

Chapter Six

ROXETTE

"Hey Ringo! Hey buddy! Hey pal!"

As soon as I stepped into the apartment, Jane threw her arms around me and squeezed. "How's it going?"

My life was getting stranger by the minute. My bald, delinquent sister, who'd never touched me in her life except to smack me, was hugging the life out of me. I was about ready to spit up a lung. Those weren't arms, they were vice grips!

"G-good," I said, embarrassed by her uncharacteristic display of affection. Mom and Dad had their arms linked around each other and they were smiling like lunatics. The whole thing reeked of some weepy Walt Disney scene. "W-when'd you get in?"

She finally released me and about a dozen silver bracelets rattled on her wrists. They matched the silver nose ring. Her jeans were slashed open across the knees, a style she'd probably drop once she felt the full brunt of the weather here. She'd left her heavy black work boots on instead of leaving them on the mat by the door where the civilized people parked theirs. And then there was that head, slick as a bowling ball.

"I got in this morning, I guess about an hour after you went to school. My flight was early."

"Imagine that!" Mom's arms flew up like the wings of a chicken. "An early flight!"

Mom always gets plucky when she's nervous. It didn't dawn on me until later that she must have taken time off work for the homecoming. She never takes time off. Work is her religion. She worships it.

"So we picked her up," Dad jumped in, "unpacked, then took her out for lunch. When we got back here we realized you'd forgotten your homework. Jane volunteered to take it."

"I was really just dying for something stronger than a cigarette," she whispered to me.

I tried not to let my face give her away. Mom and Dad would've freaked if they'd known she was still smoking pot. "So we gave her directions to the school—" Mom clucked.

"But I couldn't find it and just came back," Jane lied.

"I knew I'd see you soon enough anyway."

"Guess we'll have to give you the grand tour of the neighborhood, hey, Janie?" Dad suggested, leading us into the living room.

Jane cringed at his pet name for her. "Probably a good thing I didn't find your school," she lied a second time, and pointed to her bald head. "Your little friends might have shi—" She caught her tongue. "They might have got scared."

She pulled a package of Players Lights from her jean jacket pocket. I turned to Mom, who winced, but didn't say anything. "Where's that ashtray?" my sister asked.

Dad shot a look at Mom. He hesitated, then took our one ashtray—cheap, black plastic—out of the cupboard and set it before Jane, who'd taken over the couch.

"How was your flight?" I asked, pulling a kitchen chair over. I didn't dare sit beside her on the couch and risk getting hugged again. I needed my internal organs.

"Okay, except for the blue-haired old bag I had to sit beside. The way she kept staring you'd think she'd never seen a human being before. Plus, *she* got the window seat."

Human being? Now *that* was pushing it! Jane seemed to be doing her best to resemble anything but a human, and what she was *being* was a total jerk! I didn't really

57

care how her flight was, but I thought I'd better ease into my deeper concerns.

I wanted to know which one of us was going to get my bed, since there were only two bedrooms. I wanted to know if and when Jane was going back to school. I wanted to know if Jane had changed at all, or if she'd sneak out the door in the middle of the night, into this city she didn't know, and have Mom and Dad on the phone to the cops once again. Basically, I wanted to know who I was dealing with, and she as much as told me.

"By the way. I've changed my name." She blew a smoke ring across the room. "You can call me Roxette."

So this was how it was going to be, I thought. Jane was going to rule the roost. For one thing, there was her smoking. Smoke bothered Mom, and Dad, the health nut, despised it. Why were they letting her smoke? How would she get the money to buy them? There were no friends here to bum off of, and she'd be crazy to consider shoplifting or doing anything else that was illegal. The courts might not be so lenient if there was a next time. Plus, Mom and Dad had so little money right now. Surely *they* weren't going to buy them for her—I had trouble scoring a buck for a chocolate bar!

"Let's get some supper on," Dad suggested, "and then we can visit. How do hamburgers sound?"

"I don't know," I said. "I've never heard one."

Jane smirked, but Mom just sat there wearing a mask of concern. "Ringo?"

"Yeah, Mom?"

"Would it be okay if Jane, er, Roxette slept in your room tonight? She's had a long day."

"No problem," I said, waving my hand in front of my face for some fresh air. Mom's solution was to leave the room altogether. I decided to follow her lead. I shoulder-checked my sister, who was chipping some black nail polish off her fingernails, and flashed her a smile full of brotherly love. "Just make yourself at home."

After the hamburgers were eaten and the dishes cleared—and guess who cleared them—we sat down for a family conference. That's my Mom's language rubbing off on me again. Really, we were going to have it out.

"As you can see this apartment's not that big," Mom began, "so we're all going to have to make some compromises." Her hands were gripped firmly on her coffee cup. She hadn't drunk a drop.

Jane sighed. "Like what?"

"For one, we really can't have you smoking in here, and we'd prefer you gave it up altogether. You know it's not healthy for you, or for us to be breathing your second-hand smoke, and—"

I listened to every word, and what's more, the spaces between the words. Mom was trying so hard. Tiptoeing was not her style, but Jane might explode at any minute.

"—and you can't afford to smoke, Jane," Dad reasoned. "Plain and simple. We're trying to get on our feet again."

Smack in the middle of this ultra-serious conversation, the Beatles' *Revolution* rocked through my mind. Fitting, I thought. That's exactly what Jane was, a one-woman revolution. She jabbed out yet another cigarette, her fifth since I'd been home. There was a flurry of sparks and flying ashes.

"I'll try," she whined.

"Thank you," Mom said. She let out a long breath from her pink lungs. "Now as the house in Gibsons still hasn't sold, you and Ringo are going to have to take turns on the couch until we either get a bigger apartment or can put a down payment on a house. It's only fair."

"Ah geeeezzz," Jane and I groaned, in unison.

Then a cloud of silence filled the room. I concentrated on it and soon I could hear everyone breathe. Mom's breath was like a sigh, Jane's a tar and nicotine wheeze, and Dad's was punctuated with the odd cough and swallow. Finally, Dad smashed through the silence. "More coffee anyone?" He brought the pot to the table and topped up Mom and Jane's cups. I took another sip of juice.

"We've called the school, Dear, and you're to register tomorrow."

Jane leaned back and rolled her eyes. "School bites." Her bracelets jangled.

"We've checked it out," Mom said. "Don't judge it until you've tried it. This school has a special program for students like—"

"Like what?" Jane jumped up and her chair crashed backwards to the floor. "Like me! Don't you mean a school for *freaks* like me?"

I could see that Jane had Mom there. Just what was the politically-correct term for someone like Jane? I wondered.

"It's for students who've been out of the system and are trying to re-enter," Dad interrupted. "They have special programs and counseling—"

"Sounds just like juvy hall," Jane stormed. "I might as well have stayed in Vancouver."

Revolution was fading in and out, like the Beatles' batteries were slowly dying.

"Jane, we can't change the past," Mom continued, softening, when I bet fifty bucks she really felt like screaming, "but we can try to put it in its place. Why not give Saskatoon, and us, your family, a chance? It's not too late."

"Roxette! Call me Roxette!" When my sister's face turned red the color reached right to the top of her head. She scratched and her nails left faint white lines

61

on her skull. It would be itchy as her hair grew back.

Okay," Mom said, "it's just...hard to remember."

Jane slurped her coffee and it seemed to settle her. In a few moments she said, "Sorry for yelling." Her voice was as flat as a railroad, but the worst was over. "So what time do we have to wake up?"

It was Dad's turn again. "Uh, seven-thirty?"

"Son of a b...bird-watcher!" Jane bit it off just in time. My parents have a real thing about what they call gutter mouth.

Jane rose from the table and placed her cup in the sink. "I'm gonna crash. Night."

"Night," we called back, like a chorus, as Jane retreated to my room—*our* room. The door clicked shut and we heard boots thud against the wall.

We sat there in silence for a few moments. Mom turned the coffee cup around and around in her hands. Some of it swished out onto her knuckles, but she didn't notice. I stared at a floaty in my juice. Dad just sat and breathed, heavily, through his nostrils. Then, one by one, we each got up and began preparing for bed.

It was as if a major storm had just blown through our lives, and now that the dust had settled we had to move slowly and surely, with great faith that the sun would rise on a new day and this one would be put to rest forever.

Chapter Seven

ADJUSTING

For the next few weeks no matter where I woke up it was on the wrong side of the bed. Sleeping on the couch sucked! Ours is one of those old-fashioned couches with big buttons that dig into your skin no matter which way you squirm. Plus, the sleeping bag kept sliding off and I usually ended up on the floor. When I woke I felt like I'd gone ten rounds with a boxing champ, and lost.

"It's only temporary," Mom assured me. "Our agent says there's another family interested in the house."

She and Dad dragged me and Jane along to a couple of open houses. It was kinda fun poking around in other people's homes and seeing how they lived, and

I'm pretty sure Jane didn't steal anything.

One house reeked, like something had died in it, and the agent never even acknowledged the smell. He just kept babbling about the "newly-installed furnace," the "ready-to-be-developed family room" and the "upgraded plumbing." Mom elbowed Dad and glared at me and Jane but we couldn't stop snickering. Dad finally went into this coughing fit that could have won him an Oscar.

There'd been some close calls with Jane, a.k.a. Roxette, and Mom. I guess that's what happens when you throw a Tasmanian devil and a jack rabbit into a two-bedroom apartment. They just don't mix. There were major blowouts over Jane's poor attitude, Jane's laziness at home, and, when Mom couldn't take it another second, Jane's new look. I overheard my parents discussing it on the morning of Summer's birthday.

"She just doesn't care, Jim," Mom said, sounding tired. She was in her Saturday clothes—sloppy gray sweats and a Mickey Mouse sweatshirt—and she looked like she could sleep for a hundred days straight.

Jane walked in just at the wrong time. "Talking about me again?"

"Listen here," Mom said, "God knows I'm all for freedom of expression, but this is Saskatchewan, Jane, it's freezing out there, and your nose...it looks infected."

My sister had given up on us ever calling her Roxette. She pulled a toque over her shiny dome. "The nose ring stays," she declared, wrapping a ragged, gray scarf around her neck, "at least for now. I'm going to meet Sara at the mall." She checked her reflection in the hall mirror, then undid the chain on the door.

"We'll negotiate later," Mom said, her voice a thin, straight line.

Jane turned. "For crying out loud! My life's not a contract you can negotiate! When are you going to learn that?"

Mom opened her mouth but for once, nothing came out. Dad put his hand on her arm. "Just let her go." Jane surprised me. She didn't slam the door when she left. Even though she and Mom continued to get on each other's case, some things in my sister's life were looking up. School proved to be bearable, she'd met Sara, and I think she was staying off any cigarettes except the legal kind. More good news: she'd quit lighting up at home.

Mom took a load of dirty clothes down to the laundry room, leaving Dad and me alone. He was wearing that apron again. Pathetic. Without a job to go to, cleaning the apartment had become his career.

"So what's up for you today?" he asked. All I could see was his butt as he bent to get the dustpan in the closet.

I tried to sound casual. "Adam and I are going to a

birthday party tonight. For a girl in our class." Like it wasn't the biggest deal. "I was going to ask you and Mom...can I have a couple bucks to get her something?"

"How much is a couple?" Dad had the oldies station on the radio and began dancing with the broom to *La Bamba*.

"Fifteen?" I tried, watching him dip the broom to the floor. "Ten?"

"I think we can manage ten bucks," he said, "what do you think, Maria?" he asked the broom.

This is what being unemployed and alone in the apartment all day was doing to him. The broom was Maria; the vacuum cleaner, Tyler; our Honda Civic was Clive; and he called the television Kelly. This was a man with too much spare time.

"Maria says it's okay, but we've got to clear it with the boss first."

"Clear what with me?" Mom asked, coming in on the tail end of our conversation. She set an open roll of quarters and a box of Tide on the table. Some of the Tide spilled. A Tide pool.

"I'm going to a birthday party tonight and need to buy a gift. Is ten bucks okay?"

"I think I've got that." Mom yawned and rubbed her eyes. "I'm glad you're going out. You've been hanging around this place far too much. Do you need a ride to her house?"

"No," I said, too quickly. "Adam's Dad's driving us."

"Adam from your class?" Mom asked, wiping Tide granules off the table.

"One and the same," I answered. It wasn't like I'd made so many friends that I was likely to have two with the same name.

Mom took a ten out of her wallet and handed it to me. "How come you haven't had any of your friends over yet?" she asked.

My fingers crossed inside my pocket. "I'll bring Adam over soon." Not likely. It wasn't too likely I'd be having any visitors with this cast of clowns to embarrass me.

Now, now, Ringo…show a little respect. They are, after all, the only family you've got.

Wow. I hadn't heard from him for so long I'd almost forgotten about him.

"Who's having the party?" Mom asked.

"Summer."

"Pardon me? I thought you said summer."

"You heard right," Dad said, waltzing around our feet with Maria. "Her name's Summer.

"She's in my class, too," I blurted.

"Nice name," Mom commented. She was folding towels on the table. "Maybe you can bring her over sometime, too."

"Maybe," I said, and added to myself when hell freezes over, the cows come home, pigs fly, Jane's hair grows back and Dad stops dancing with the broom. Never.

After lunch I walked to Adam's house. He lives on Spadina Crescent, a long, winding street that runs beside the South Saskatchewan River. He'd told me about the bike trails in the valley along the river and said we'd have to hit them as soon as the snow melted and the trails dried. "You can ride for miles and not even know you're in a city," he promised. He said that sometimes garter snakes slithered across the bike path, and once he'd seen a weasel being chased by a bunch of magpies. Cool!

I'd been to Adam's a few times. A regular house, regular family. His little brother and sister were video game addicts; his parents both worked full time. Nothing but normal. I wondered what it was like.

Adam's dad dropped us off at the mall and soon after we ran into Tori and Karen, who were also shopping for Summer's gift. They must have been through the perfume testers; we could smell them coming. "I got her a friendship ring," Tori said, showing us a ring that split into halves. Man, it was ugly!

"Nice," Adam and I said together. "Pop jinx!"

We left the girls and went into a bookstore. Adam picked up a plain paper journal with a flowery fabric cover. "Hey, you know how Summer's into writing poetry and stuff. She'd love this," Adam said, turning it over. "And it's only $7.99."

He bought the journal and we joined the mall traffic again. "I don't know what to get," I complained. "Really, I hardly know Summer."

"What about the school dance?" Adam asked. "It looked to me like you were getting to know her very well."

I blushed at the memory. "Yeah, but it's not like we're going out or anything." We were still kinda shy around each other at school. Plus, I concentrated most of my school energy on dodging whatever Larry was letting fly—personal insults, sharp pencils—you name it. It didn't matter what I did or didn't do, the guy just seemed to have it in for me. I know I wasn't imagining it, because even Ms. Harmon had asked if I knew why Larry was so mean to me. I couldn't give her an answer and she said sometimes there is no answer, at least not anything a guy can see on the surface. Sometimes a problem's buried so deep it would take an archaeologist to dig to the truth.

"We're running out of time, Ringo," Adam reminded me as we stopped to plug a gumball machine.

I had to re-focus. "You've gone to school with her forever, Adam. What does she like?"

"Well she used to collect teddy bears," he said. He blew a big blue bubble and it popped in his face. "Probably still does."

"Teddy bears?"

"You know," he kidded, "those brown fuzzy things with four legs. Why not get her one?"

I swear I checked out every stuffed animal in the entire mall. Those things were not cheap! "The only thing under ten bucks is this one," I whined. I held up a small brown bear with glossy black eyes, curly hair and a red ribbon around its neck. "It's so plain."

"If it's from you, she'll love it," Adam reassured me, checking his watch.

"You think so?"

"Ringo, it's taken you two hours to find this. Buy it, then we're outta here. I'm dying for a Coke."

I wasn't convinced. "You're sure she'd like it?"

Adam sighed. "You can sue me if she doesn't. Come on, Ringo, you said it yourself, I've known her forever. I also know she likes you. It's basically a no-fail situation." He pushed me toward the cash register.

"Cool," I said, my blood rushing to my cheeks as I paid for the bear. With tax included, I had just enough left for a pop.

We were scanning the food court for an empty table when Adam grabbed my sleeve and said, "Quick, this way."

"What's going on?" I asked, but it was too late. Larry had seen us, and he was closer. He was alone, which was no surprise; the guy couldn't buy a friend. There was nothing to do but wait for his abuse. I might lose my pride but I sure hoped to keep all my teeth. I held the teddy bear in front of me as if it were bulletproof.

"So what'd you get your girlfriend?" he asked, strutting toward me. His snotty voice made my skin crawl.

"A teddy bear," I answered.

"Wooo hoooo. A teddy bear! Last of the big-time spenders." Several heads turned to his abrasive voice.

Adam rolled his eyes. "Let's fly Ringo. We've got places to go, people to meet." He tugged my sleeve and although I thought my legs were frozen in place, they actually did their job and got me out of there.

"See you tonight, girls," Larry called after us.

"Did he have to be so loud?" I asked Adam. "Half the people in the food court were gawking at us."

Adam kept walking straight ahead, chin up. "Tonight, just remember...strength in numbers."

Chapter Eight

SUMMER'S PARTY - PART I

I screwed up on Summer's gift. Who knew wrapping a teddy bear was impossible? I ripped the paper and we were out of tape so I had to use bandages! Real subtle. I didn't even have a bow to hide the flaws. Then I folded some wrapping paper in half and made a flimsy card. I threw the whole mess in a bag and met Adam at his place.

"So what do you do at parties here?" I asked, that ball in my stomach shifting. Summer's house was only a few minutes from Adam's.

Adam chucked a snowball and nailed a stop sign. "Eat, listen to music, dance, play Truth or Dare. You know."

"Oh." Exactly what we did in Gibsons. "Do you think we will tonight?"

"Will what?"

"Play Truth or Dare."

"Yup."

Gulp. I felt like ditching the bear and using the bag to breathe into. Tonight I might kiss Summer! I wished I had some gum or breath mints. I'd brushed and flossed my teeth, but one never knew. My emotions and hormones were running wild. On the one hand, I was having visions of kissing Summer, but on the other I was dreading what Larry might have in store for me. Why did everything in life have a flipside? Side A and Side B.

"Here we are," Adam announced, and before you could say "chicken out" Summer was opening the front door for us. She had on a seventies-style dress, with a high waist and a daisy design. *Very* hip.

"Everyone's downstairs," she explained, taking my bag and the perfectly-wrapped gift out of Adam's hands while we unlaced our boots. "Follow me."

She added the gifts to the pile on the living room coffee table and we followed her through the kitchen, past a reasonably normal-looking adult whom I assumed was her mother, and down the stairs.

"I thought we were going to be early," Adam said, surprised to see that the super large, rectangular room was already packed with partygoers.

It felt like New Year's Eve, not that I've ever been to a New Year's Eve bash, but I can imagine. The music was blaring. Colorful streamers and bunches of balloons dangled from the ceiling. At one end of the long room, Matt, Steven, Keith and Ben were playing a rowdy game of ping-pong while Bobby B. watched. There were couches and chairs and a gas fireplace at the other end, where Leanne, Christy, Lisa, Jalynne, Vanessa, Bailey and Amanda were sitting cross-legged on the rug. I congratulated myself for remembering all their names.

"There's still more people coming!" Tori was even more hyper than usual, like a two-year-old who doesn't know the meaning of *relax*. She'd outlined her eyes with eyeliner and had gone totally overboard with mascara and blue eye shadow. The mascara was running and she'd gone up too high over her eyes with the eye shadow. She was a ringer for a character from *Star Trek*.

She and Summer were setting bowl after bowl on a long table against one wall—chips, dip, nachos, peanuts, hard candies, soft candies, popcorn and other goodies—it was a junk food buffet!

"Well, we're not going to starve," Adam stated, popping a nacho into his mouth. Apparently he didn't care about bad breath.

Summer's mom teetered downstairs cradling three bottles of pop and more glasses. She had short, wavy hair and didn't look very old, but just then she had that frazzled look that all moms get. "Could someone give me a hand?" I took the bottles, setting them beside the others already on the table.

"Thanks," she said, "I don't think we've met. You must be Ringo." She offered her hand and I shook it, firmly, like my parents taught me to. "Summer's told me about you."

"How do you do?" I asked, amazed that it actually came out right. "Nice house," I said, glancing around. Small talk is not one of my strong points.

"Thanks." She ran a hand across her forehead, like she'd just completed a marathon.

"Mom, where's the cake?" Summer was beside me. I could see the resemblance between mother and daughter. It was in the eyes.

"The cake!" Her mother sprinted upstairs and Summer and I turned to each other, laughing.

"Mothers!" she said. "What's your Mom like?"

I thought for a moment, searching for the most accurate word. "Busy."

Someone shrieked in soprano. "Summer!"

Two unfamiliar guys and two girls came thundering toward us. Summer hugged the girls while I stood there like a wooden puppet with a phoney grin painted on my face. "Ringo," she said, "meet my friends. Travis, Desire, Sherae and Joel."

I said hello to each of them, instantly forgetting their names if I'd even heard them properly to start with.

Summer was wearing her season on her face. "We're in drama together."

"So this is *that* Ringo," Sherae said, her voice rising and falling like a kite in the wind.

Summer blushed. I blushed. Did they know something I didn't?

"We've heard all about you," Desire, the tall redhead, said.

"Yes," Joel said, teasing, "*all* about you."

They seemed like a fun bunch. Fun, and hungry, too. After introductions they stormed the food table and I had a moment alone with Summer.

"I didn't know you were in drama," I said.

"I guess we have a lot to learn about each other," she replied, "but tonight probably won't be the time or place."

Jolly good, Ringo. Jolly good.

"Probably not," I agreed. The noise level was worse than in the school hallway on Fridays at 3:30.

"Hi guys!" Tori bounced up to us. "We're just waiting for a few more people."

Even more? I wondered where they'd find room.

"Help yourself to some food," Summer offered, "as you can see, Mom went out of control." A huge teddy bear cake with chocolate icing and white candles had been added to the buffet table.

"Let's go get the rest of those gifts," Tori, the organizer, said, pulling Summer toward the stairs.

I scanned the room for Adam. He was hanging out at the table tennis game, where another loud cheer threatened to raise the roof.

"The winners!" Matt yelled, high-fiving Steven.

"We'll take you on," Adam challenged.

"You and who?" Matt wondered. "Ringo Starr?"

"Yeah. Back in Gibsons Ringo was the ping-pong champion at his school. Right, Ringo?"

I raised my eyebrows. Wrong. I wasn't the champion of anything, anywhere. "Thanks a lot pal," I whispered, taking my paddle and my place at the end of the table.

We beat Matt and Steven 21-19. I was so busy watching that bouncing white ball that I didn't notice when Larry arrived, followed by Jesse, Shawn, Logan, Johnathon and Craig. They mingled with the girls by the fireplace.

"Okay everyone," Tori shouted above the music. "Time to open gifts!"

Summer looked like she'd rather not have been the center of attention. Tori had her sitting on a chair in front of the fireplace while the rest of us stared on. The presents just kept coming. There was socks, CDs, hair accessories, a T-shirt, cash in cards, a pair of silver earrings, three necklaces and a book of poetry. Adam's journal went over big.

It must have been awful for Summer, having to sit there, smile nonstop, and thank everyone, like at a shower or the gift opening after a wedding. I'd never been at a birthday bash like this before. I'm surprised Tori didn't write down who brought what, and then it hit me—soon Summer would come to my stupid gift. I should have opted for a necklace, or earrings. Anything but that cheap teddy bear.

"Whatsa matter, Ringo?" Larry asked, his sour cream and onion breath warming the side of my face. I didn't realize he'd been stalking me. "You're lookin' a little green around the gills."

Don't let him get to you, Ringo. You haven't got anything to be embarrassed about.

Tori passed Summer another present. "What could this be?" she wondered, studying the large, wrapped box on her lap. She carefully pulled apart the wrapping paper to reveal a white gift box. The taped corners came off with a pop.

"Oh my God!" Summer squealed.

Whatever was underneath was hidden from us by the lid. The people closest moved in and then we were all stretching on our tiptoes as Summer pulled the gift out.

"Who...who...?" she stammered.

"My God! A leather jacket!" Tori exclaimed. "Who's it from?"

Jalynne knelt down and dug in the papers on the rug. "Here's the card!" She opened it and then yelled: "Ringo!"

First there was a moment of silence, like in the gym on Remembrance Day. Then Summer waded through the gift wrap and gave me a major hug—in front of everyone. "You shouldn't have!" she shouted, crushing me, "but I'm so glad you did. I love it! It's just the best gift ever!"

"But I...I," She released me and I glanced at Adam, who raised his palms in wonder. What was going on? Summer slipped on the black leather jacket. It looked soft and smooth and worth major cash-ola. Mom told me that you can tell real leather by the smell. I was dying to sniff, but resisted. It really looked hot on her, with her golden hair, but I couldn't let her think it was from me! "Summer, I should tell you that..."

Everyone was stroking the leather, oohing and awing. Summer couldn't hear me above the admiration.

"You'll never know how much this means to me, Ringo." Her top lip started to tremble. "Thank you so much."

"But I need to tell you—"

"Don't say a word!" Summer cried. "I have to show Mom!" She took the stairs three at a time.

Eventually Tori got things settled down again. One moment I was hearing the crowd roar and the next I was lost in the second verse of *Strawberry Fields Forever*. When I snapped out of it, Summer'd come back downstairs and Tori was ordering her to open the last gift.

"We almost forgot it!" Tori announced.

I should be so lucky, I thought to myself. I should have kidnapped the bear when everyone was praising the jacket.

I backed off to a corner. Summer, in her new leather jacket, picked up my rumpled gift. The little teddy bear rolled to the rug. "Oh, it's adorable," she claimed. She turned the bear over, as if looking for a card. It was gone! In place of my makeshift card was an envelop that no doubt held a real card. But from who? I waited, breathless, while she read. Then: "Thanks, Larry. It'll go great with my collection."

Larry! So that's what he did! He switched our gifts! He'd be the only one who could afford a leather jacket, or, knowing his reputation, have the nerve to steal one, but why would he want to make me look good by signing my name to it and his to the teddy bear? Why would anyone pull such a thing?

"Let's pick teams for Twister," Tori yelled above the commotion. She began clearing a space for the plastic game sheet. Bailey and Amanda were helping Summer move the gifts to her bedroom, which was directly off the large rumpus room.

I watched Larry grab a ping-pong paddle from Bobby B. and bully his way into a game. I'd just stay clear, for now. I caught up with Adam by the chip bowl. "What is going on?"

"Your guess is as good as mine. What are you going

to do?" He munched between his words.

"I tried to tell her, but—"

"Here, you need a drink." Adam pressed a glass of Sprite into my hand. I downed it in one gulp. My throat burned.

"He's up to something," I wheezed.

Just then Larry whacked Jesse with the paddle. Travis's orange pop went flying, hitting Leanne in the face. The pop stained the carpet. Leanne threw her arms up and accidentally bumped Keith, who was carrying a bowl of buttered popcorn. Shawn and Johnathon bonked heads as they both bent to pick it up. Tori was running around with paper towels, trying to clean the wet, sticky mess. Logan tripped across her and got a bad rug burn on his elbow. Someone cranked the music and a group of girls started to dance. A bunch of guys began moshing. Ben was jiving with Lisa. The drama group was playing charades. The music and noise were so loud I thought for sure Summer's mom would freak.

"What a circus!" I yelled to Adam.

He was laughing at something Vanessa had just said. "What's that?"

"I said...what a circus!"

There was an ear-splitting crash. Craig and Jesse, who were wrestling over a Frisbee, had fallen against the buffet table. What they didn't know was that it was a folding table. With collapsible legs. The teddy bear cake and everything else splattered onto the floor.

"You think *this* is something?" Adam shouted. "The night, my friend, is young."

Chapter Nine

SUMMER'S PARTY - PART II: TRUTH OR DARE

We eventually got the mess cleaned up. Summer's mom came thundering down stairs when she heard the crash, and she was not a happy camper. We all tried to pitch in. Adam kept muttering as he scrubbed root beer out of the rug. He'd cut his hand on a broken glass and blood dripped onto his jeans. Christy tried to salvage some of the cake, but Summer has a cat, Sasha, a Persian that sheds long white hair, and after the cake had been scraped off the floor, well, let's just say it wasn't very appetizing. Mind you, that didn't stop Larry from filling his disgusting face with it.

"Hey, Ringo!" he yelled, his mouth full of chocolate

cake and white cat hair. "You ever seen sea food?" He showed me the half-chewed mush in his mouth.

"You're sickening!" Bailey cried.

Larry pulled a long white hair through his teeth. "Dental floss, anyone?"

Several partygoers groaned.

It wasn't long before the crowd split into groups. Some turned themselves into human pretzels playing Twister, others competed at ping-pong, some danced, and a few were standing around the telephone looking guilty. A handful of people were hanging out near the up-righted food table and others disappeared behind a door into another room.

"Are you in?" Adam asked. He was heading for the door and the mystery behind it.

"In for what?" Like I didn't suspect.

"Truth or Dare. We're playing in the storage room."

I followed my friend into the dark storage and laundry room. Only a single candle was burning. Summer, Tori, Matt, Keith, Shawn, Amanda and Karen were sitting in a circle on the floor. Matt was huddled up beside Summer.

"Okay, let's start," Tori commanded. Adam and I squeezed in between Shawn and Amanda, who began chanting, "Truth, dare, double dare, promise to repeat."

"Summer goes first," Matt said, "'cause it's her birthday."

"No, someone else start," Summer protested. "Ringo, why don't you go first?"

Oh great, I thought, what a position to be in. I decided to attack Matt. Maybe I could get Larry off my case and onto Matt's.

"Matt, I dare you to call Larry a loser."

"That's not fair," Matt griped. "We have to stay in this room."

"What kind of rule is that?" Adam asked.

"House rules," Tori said.

I noticed that Summer didn't say anything about house rules and it was her house, but I didn't push it. "Okay," I said, wracking my brain for something equally brilliant. "I dare you to...drip candle wax on your arm."

Matt grabbed the candle. "That's a sissy dare," he said. He tipped the candle and a drop of wax plopped onto his skin. The hair on his arm sizzled. "Ouch!"

"Your face is beet red!" Shawn shouted.

Matt peeled the wax off and Amanda inspected his arm. "I took the babysitting course and I learned that if—"

"I'm fine," Matt cut her off. "Let's keep playing."

"We have to go in a circle," Karen insisted. "Adam, it's your turn."

"I dare..." he hesitated, building the suspense, "Keith to kiss Tori."

I let out a long breath. I was safe. Keith kissed Tori

on the cheek. She singed the ends of her hair when she bent across the candle's flame.

Then it was Shawn's turn. "Karen, is it true that you like Steven?"

Karen pushed her hair behind her ears. "No way!"

"Come on, Karen," Amanda urged, "you have to tell the truth."

"Well I used to, but now I like Devon Archer. You don't know him. He doesn't go to West Park."

"I know him!" Keith yelped. "We're on the same ball team. He's about three feet shorter than you! You'd have to cut your legs off to look him in the eye!"

Matt and Amanda laughed.

"Okay, next," Tori said, keeping the game rolling. "Keith's up."

Keith looked at Summer, then at Matt. "I double dare Summer to kiss Matt."

Oooh, daggers to my heart! I didn't want to watch, but it was sorta like driving by an accident—I just had to look. Matt slung his arm around Summer and pulled her toward him. One quick kiss on the lips. Summer didn't close her eyes and didn't look like she was too excited about the whole thing, but Matt's head seemed to get a bit bigger. Maybe it was just my imagination, but I'd like to believe that she didn't even pucker.

"Now me," Tori said. "I doggy dare Adam to stand in the shower with all his clothes on."

"But we can't leave the room," Adam tried.

"You don't have to," Tori explained, "the shower's right back there." She pointed to a corner of the storage room. Matt stood and flicked on the light. Sure enough, there was a toilet, a sink, a mirror and a single shower stall.

"Dad always said he was going to build walls," Summer said. Her voice dropped an octave. "That's just one more thing he lied about."

"Do I have to?" Adam asked. "I'll freeze."

"It's a doggy dare," Matt said. "You have to."

We followed Adam to the shower. He pulled back the curtain and turned on the tap. "Oooh, that's cold!" he whimpered, testing the water with his hand.

"The hot water doesn't work very well down here," Summer revealed. "Sorry."

"Dive in," Matt said, giving Adam a push, "while we count to ten."

He stayed under the water for the count then jumped back out.

"You should have stayed in for twenty!" Matt shouted. "Ten's easy."

It didn't matter. My friend was soaked and moments later, shivering. Summer grabbed a bath towel from the top of the dryer. "Here," she said, pushing it toward him. She glared at Matt. "That was cruel."

We returned to our circle on the floor. The lights were turned back off and the candle's flame flickered.

We could hear laughter, voices and music in the big room next door. Summer was looking right at me, even through me, but then she dared Amanda to kiss Matt. Amanda did.

Matt was getting altogether too much action for my liking. I was batting zero. I was wondering if I'd ever get in on the game, then Matt came up with an outrageous dare for me.

"I doggy dare Ringo to shave off his eyebrows," he said.

"I'm sure!" Summer tried. "Ringo, you don't have to."

"Yes he does," Matt argued, and Keith, Tori and Amanda agreed.

"I...I wouldn't even know how!" I sputtered.

"Well, look what I found by the sink," Matt said, pulling a razor out of his back pocket. "Just lather up with some soap and water, and then," he swiped the razor through the air, inches above his own eyebrows, "zip—you're done."

Oh this is special, I thought. My first time at a party with my new friends and some jerk wants me to prove myself by shaving off my brows!

"Come on, Ringo, it's only hair. It'll grow back." Keith wasn't very encouraging. "I did it myself two months ago and see," he parted his bangs, "they came back just like before."

Beside me, Adam's teeth were chattering. The wet

clothes stuck to his goose-pimpled skin. "S-stand up to h-him," he encouraged. He looked terrible. *He* might catch pneumonia for his deed, and all I had to do was shave off my eyebrows. If I did it right, it shouldn't even hurt.

"Okay, I'll do it," I said. The lights went back on and everyone crowded around me as I stood before the bathroom, well, the not-quite-a-bathroom mirror. I lathered my eyebrows and slowly lifted the razor. "Here goes!"

I was surprised at how easily they came off, and what a clean job I made of it. I looked at my new self in the mirror. Now *I* was the freak from *Star Trek*! Wow, did I look stupid. Shawn, Tori, Amanda, Keith and Matt were killing themselves laughing. I couldn't face Summer.

"Well, I must say you've won my respect." Matt slapped me on the back as we sat back down.

"Uh...thanks, I guess." I tried to pull my bangs forward, but my hair wasn't cut right for bangs so there was no hiding my new look.

Then, the dare I'd been waiting for all night happened. Amanda dared me to kiss Summer! Everyone hooted. I hoped my breath was okay; too late now to change it. I wondered how we were going to manage this. Summer was across the circle from me. There was another long pause, like in church after a prayer. They were waiting, staring at me. I felt naked.

What are you waiting for? This is your big moment. Chop chop.

I swallowed hard. "Let's stand up," I suggested. The voice didn't sound like my own. Summer stood and stepped toward me, those green eyes sparkling in the candlelight. I put my hands on her shoulders and was slowly closing in on her lips when the door burst open and all hell broke loose!

"Yeehaw!" Larry yelled, swinging something in the air like a cowboy with a lasso. A screaming mob crashed into the storage room behind him and we scooted out of the way to avoid being trampled. Logan and Ben were trying to grab whatever it was Larry was swinging. All the girls were hollering. It was a stampede, and Larry was a bull on the loose!

Tori was first to reach the light switch.

"It's a double-barreled slingshot!" Larry wailed.

"Oh my God, it's Summer's bra!" Karen screamed. "He snuck into her room and stole her bra! Get him!"

I felt my blood boil, and the chase was on. Larry bolted back through the door into the big room, where he kept jumping over furniture, shouting and swinging the bra around and around.

"It's Summer's over-the-shoulder-boulder-holder!" he wailed, waving it like a flag.

Summer had crumpled into a corner by the fireplace, her face hidden behind her hands. I was so embarrassed for her I could have died.

We eventually rounded Larry up and kicked him out. Some of the guys even continued chasing him down the street, but it didn't matter anymore; the damage had been done. That bra had gone flying around the room at least a dozen times.

Summer's mom marched downstairs and said the party was definitely over. She and Tori escorted Summer, her shoulders slumped in shame, into her bedroom and closed the door.

"Quite a party," I said to Adam as we ambled down the cold, dark street away from Summer's humiliation. The snow crunched beneath our boots. I thought I felt the place where my eyebrows used to be starting to freeze.

Adam was walking stiff-legged. His jeans had frozen solid and the pant legs were slapping back and forth against each other. His hair had hardened into a peculiar crown.

"Mmmm. Not b-bad," he stuttered, then we looked at each other and for some reason we started to laugh.

I knew it was wrong, like laughing in church or when you hear someone's uncle died, but we just couldn't stop it. Sure we felt terrible for Summer, but when the laughter burst forth like water through a dam it felt so good we both just let it go and I almost forgot I'd just missed kissing Summer. Almost, but not quite.

Chapter Ten

BULL'S EYE

Mom and Dad were not impressed. A bald daughter and now an eyebrow-deficient son. Our hairlessness was the first thing Jane and I'd had in common for a long time.

I got grounded for two weeks—no TV or anything—so thought it would be a good time to write my buddy, Jeff, back in Gibsons. I told him all about Summer, school, and of course, the party. Summer hadn't even come to school on the following Monday. On Tuesday she looked so broken I didn't dare hurt her even more by telling her the truth about the leather jacket. The lie was like a wound that was beginning to fester inside me. I just had to wait for the right time to confess and then hope that she'd still speak to me.

"So that's where my love life is at," I wrote. "How's yours? Is Mandy still calling you and hanging up? Is Shannon still going out with Kevin, or has she finally cut him off?"

It was a very long letter, and I wrote it all on the can, since that was the only place where I could get any privacy.

Dad was still not working, and, grounded or not, he made me go grocery shopping with him. In SuperValu, the Beatles' hit, *Hey Jude*, came on over the speakers. So what does Dad do? He starts singing along at the top of his lungs using a banana as a microphone! Eyeballs started popping out of heads. I thought security was going to haul him away! I got out of produce, real fast, and waited for him by the soup section.

Apparently I wasn't fast enough. Leanne, in my class, saw the whole thing. Word got around and Larry made the most of it. He squashed a rotten banana on the seat of my desk and I didn't see it until it was too late. I looked like I'd...well, you know.

One afternoon Mom came home with great news. "Someone bought our old house!" This sent us into a real estate frenzy, but I think we came out of it all with a good deal. We'd soon be moving into a two-storey brick house, not far from West Park. It had a verandah, fireplace, sunroom and *four* bedrooms with a balcony off the master.

At school, everyone was talking about Ms. Harmon. She hadn't been herself for weeks and even I, the new kid, had noticed.

"She used to be so nice," Summer reflected. "So happy."

It was recess, and we'd meandered to a distant corner of the schoolyard, far away from all playground activity, the curious eyes of our classmates and Larry's ruthless slingshot. Human beings made excellent targets for his whizzing rocks. He wasn't supposed to have a slingshot at school, but he'd managed to hide it from the teachers and everyone was too chicken to rat on him. I'm sure he loved recess.

The snow had been disappearing in fits and starts. I found a rare patch of dry, dusty grass, and Summer and I plopped down on it. It was pretty decent out but she was still wearing her leather jacket; she rarely took it off. "I know what you mean," I replied, agreeing about the radical change in Ms. Harmon. "She freaked on Jesse for handing in his math assignment a day late!"

"I couldn't believe it. I'd never even heard her raise her voice before," Summer continued. She stretched out on her side, supporting herself on one elbow. "Don't tell anyone," she urged, plucking a piece of dead grass from the ground, "but last week after school I had to come back to get my runners and I found her at her desk, crying."

"Really?" I stretched to pick a sliver of grass just as Summer did, and when our hands met my heart flipped like a diver off a spring board. "What happened?"

"She pretended it was just her allergies acting up, but it wasn't, Ringo." Summer searched the perfect, cloudless sky, as if for answers. "Something is seriously wrong."

Well, something may have been wrong with Ms. Harmon, but aside from Larry's occasional humiliations, everything was coming up sweet in my life. Summer and I were spending tons of time together at school and we'd also had some long talks on the telephone.

Alexander Graham Bell must have been in love when he invented the phone. Maybe he was a little like me. I've always found it easier to talk to people, especially girls, through the safety of a telephone line. I don't have to worry about where to look, or fret about what they may be seeing when they look at me.

Time dissolved when Summer and I gabbed. We'd talk about everything from bears to baseball and back again. Food was often a starting point for these conversations. We'd relive our day through our stomachs. Summer loved Alphabits. I was a Raisin Bran man.

Summer gave me the goods on Matt, whom she'd been in school with since kindergarten. She'd never liked him except as a friend, which put my trembling heart at ease. She'd gone to a show at the Broadway Theatre with him once and after that everyone thought they were going out. Especially Matt. She also confessed that she was the one who'd brought the Beatles CD to the dance. "Because of your name," she confided. "I thought you'd figure it out." And guess who requested the slow song, our first dance together? Ahhhhh.

I knew it was time to come clean about the jacket. I'd also tell Summer about my sister, Jane, and confess that she was the one who'd come to the school after the Valentine's Dance. I felt better, just having decided to tell the truth. I dialed the number and Summer answered, but before I could get the load off *my* chest, she had one to get off hers.

"I want to tell you about my father," she said. "My counselor says it's important to talk about it."

Counselor? I guessed Summer'd been damaged more than I thought by her father's affair and the family split, but I should have known—he was the subject of all of her hate poems.

"You're probably wondering why he's not living with us anymore," she continued.

Sure, I was curious about what'd happened.

"He's an accountant," she began. "Every spring since I can remember, he's worked long hours during tax season. It was normal. We didn't think anything of it."

I sprawled across the couch, listening carefully to

every word, and hit the stopwatch function on my watch. I'd started timing our calls, and I knew this would be a record-breaker.

"First, let me take you back," she said. "Once upon a time we were happy. That's why it hurt so much. My parents didn't fight, except about the usual stuff, and I thought I was one of the lucky ones...you know, to still have both my mother and father living with me. We did things together. Camping, movies, anything. Most of my friends' parents are split up. I should have known my luck would run out sooner or later."

She seemed to have forgotten that I was on the other end of the line, because she just kept talking, like it was rehearsed.

"Last year, during tax season, I was downtown with Tori when I got this idea to stop by Dad's office. I'd hardly seen him for weeks. Tori said she had to get home anyway, so I went on my own. It was a great day. I wanted to see if he'd take a break, maybe have an ice-cream cone with me on the riverbank. The door to his office wasn't locked so I walked right in. He, uh, he wasn't alone."

"Oh," I said.

"He'd been lying to me and Mom for months."

"Oh." I didn't want to get into it. Too personal for this cat.

"I'll never get that picture out of my head." Summer sniffed, and I wished I could stretch my arms through the phone line and hold her, but of course, I didn't say that.

"Summer? Are you okay?"

She sniffed again. "I can't stand liars! He ruined everything! Everything! You can't imagine what it's like. This had been going on for *years*."

I eventually got her calmed down, but there was no one to calm *my* shattered nerves. She hated liars! Once again, this was not going to be the right time to confess anything.

"Ringo, the bell!" Summer stood and brushed the grass off her jeans. I truly hadn't heard the bell ring us back in from recess, or noticed the little kids leaving the slides and their chicken fights at the monkey bars to file back into school.

We were almost at the door when something cracked against the back of my skull. A bullet of pain knocked me to my knees. "What the—?"

I didn't need to turn around. I knew Larry would be skulking behind some corner, his slingshot stuffed beneath his bulky sweater. I touched the stinging spot and my fingers came back red.

"My God, Ringo!" Summer surveyed the damage. "It's bleeding pretty bad. You might need stitches!"

I was standing again but at the mention of stitches I felt woozy and stumbled. It was like I'd just stepped off the Zipper at the summer fair.

Summer pulled the scrunchy from her braid and pressed it against the wound. "Keep steady pressure on it," she advised, as we zigzagged toward the school.

Inside, Summer ran ahead to get Ms. Harmon. I was getting weaker by the second, and flopped near the boot racks, my head throbbing. The next thing I knew Summer and Ms. Harmon were helping me down the hall to the office. I had to put my arm around Summer's shoulders, to steady myself. Ms. Harmon had a good grip on my elbow. Adam was bringing up the rear, wiping drops of my blood off the floor.

"Larry did this," Summer declared, before I had a chance to stop her. "He's got a slingshot and he's shooting rocks at everyone."

"Are you sure?" Ms. Harmon asked.

"Positive," Adam cut in. "I saw him do it."

I was pretty dozy, but I know I heard Ms. Harmon right. "He'll pay for this," she said, her voice like black coffee. "He'll pay."

We arrived at the office and the secretary scrambled to unlock the first aid supplies. "She'll call your Dad," Ms. Harmon said. "You should have this checked out by a doctor."

"Catch you later, Ringo." Adam looked concerned.

I stepped toward an orange chair, forgetting that I was still linked to Summer.

"Uh, Ringo? I need my arm back."

"Oh. Sorry." I reluctantly let go. "Thanks for your help."

"Hey, what are girlfriends for?" she answered. "Talk to you soon."

My heart, like my head, swelled.

The secretary cleaned me up a bit, then gave me an ice pack and called Dad. Back home, I got two Tylenol and the third degree.

"Is there something you haven't been telling us?" Dad asked. There wasn't a speck of humor in his voice.

"No," I said. I was hoping the Tylenol would kick in soon. I was getting a massive headache. "It was just an accident."

"An accident! Some guy beans you with a rock fired from a slingshot and you're sticking up for him? What's wrong with you?"

I swallowed hard, hating myself for the coward I was becoming. "Nothing's wrong. You know, boys will be boys and all that."

"Well that Larry is one boy who's going to be sorry he ever owned a slingshot!" Dad fumed. "I'm going to be talking to your teacher *and* his parents about this."

"Dad, really—" I started, but it was already too late. He was on the phone.

Summer called after school. I ran the long telephone cord under the bathroom door for a private talk and got the grim news. "Ms. Harmon sent Larry to Mrs.

Krause's office. He's been suspended for three days."

"Oh no," I grumbled, my thoughts slipping off my tongue like water.

"What'd you say?" Summer asked.

"It's just that he's going to hate me even more now," I griped, hoping she wouldn't sense how terrified I really was.

"Don't worry about it. He hates everyone," she said, trying to reassure me.

"Yeah, but for some reason he seems to hate me the most, and now I'm doomed," I confessed. "Dad called his parents."

"And?"

"They're in Jamaica. On holidays."

"And they left Larry here?"

"Guess so," I quipped. "I guess his ancient grandma's been staying with him."

"Geez," Summer replied, "that really sucks."

There were a few moments of silence while I suspect that Summer, like me, was rolling everything over in her mind. Then she said, "I'm still curious about Ms. Harmon and what's been bothering her."

"I can't imagine," I answered, never guessing that Larry might be the cause of something even bigger than the lump on my head.

Chapter Eleven

A FAMILY AFFAIR

My head was still throbbing the next day, but I managed to drag myself into class anyway. Someone had written a limerick on the board:

> There once was a bully named Larry
> Who everyone thought was quite scary
> His hobby was crime
> He was mean all the time
> And he'd kill if you called him a fairy!

Ms. Harmon erased it as soon as she came in, but not before everyone recognized Adam's handwriting. He and Summer passed me cheery notes all morning, trying to keep my spirits up. Ms. Harmon seemed too preoccupied to notice.

When the noon bell rang, Adam invited me over for lunch. I tried not to think about the pain as I dodged puddles with my good friend and girlfriend on either side.

Girlfriend. I liked the sound of that. And Summer had even said it, so I wasn't making it up! Not a friend who's a girl, I'd had lots of those, but a *girlfriend*. There was a major difference. A girl who's a friend doesn't hold your hand when you're walking down the street. She doesn't tell you that she sleeps with your school picture tucked under her pillow. Being around an ordinary friend doesn't make you nervous and deliriously happy at the same time. It doesn't make you sweat.

We walked with a warm, welcome breeze at our backs.

"Hey guys, look!" Summer squinted at the sky. "The sun's a giant lemon pie!"

I looked up. The sun was giving off some serious rays. I know you're not supposed to stare at it, but sometimes I do, just to make sure everything in the universe is still in the right place. I do the same thing with the moon, and the Big Dipper, and Orion, only they don't hurt my eyes and make me see pink and orange spots.

"Man, when spring finally arrives in Saskatoon, it arrives in a big way," I said.

A few days before we'd been in winter coats and boots and now we could almost break out the shorts!

Summer'd gathered her golden hair into a ponytail that bounced as she walked. She'd tied her windbreaker around her waist. Finally, something other than that leather jacket, which was like a fist in the gut each time I saw it. If Larry'd exchanged our gifts just to hurt me, he'd succeeded.

As we got closer to the river we saw a few keeners running along the paved trail and an old guy on roller blades cruising with his dog.

"Let's check out the weir," Adam suggested, and before we knew it he was halfway across Spadina Crescent.

"What's a weir?" I asked. The word wasn't in my vocabulary.

"You'll see," Summer said.

We waited for three cars to pass, then jogged hand in hand across the street to the river. Several people were gathered near a set of blue binoculars on a pole. A couple guys were going crazy with their cameras.

"That's a weir," Summer advised me. We leaned against the chain-link fence beside Adam and Summer pointed down the steep cement embankment to where the South Saskatchewan tumbled over a man-made waterfall. The water was a mirror of calm before the weir, but it hissed and splashed and protested after it tumbled over. It was as if the river was trying to say something, but the message was garbled.

"Sometimes I like to come down here and write

poems," Summer said. "It's a good place to think about things."

Five huge white birds with big, scooped bills bobbed into the swirling water.

"Pelicans," Adam said. "You should take a closer look." He got into the line-up for the binoculars, but I stayed back with Summer.

That was the first time I heard it, a sound that started out low, like a woman humming, then grew into something steady and strong. "Listen," I said.

Summer turned to me. "What am I listening for?"

"Don't you hear anything?"

"Sure. Pelicans, people, cars on Spadina."

"No, something else."

She closed her eyes, then shook her head. Maybe I was the only one who could hear it. I didn't think there was any more room inside my head, what with the Beatles singing and that inner voice yakking, but I heard it in there, too. Above all that other noise, I heard the river roar.

A familiar voice shattered the moment. "Hey, Ringo! Ringo!"

No, I thought, couldn't be. I dropped Summer's hand. "Ringo...who's that?" she whispered as the runner came closer. Adam was also curious. He'd left the line-up and wandered over.

The big man loped toward us, then stopped. "Hi, Dad," I said, flatly. He'd fallen behind in his training.

He was wheezing. Adam and Summer exchanged glances.

"Well hello, kiddo. You're not skipping out are you?" His eyes kept darting from me to my friends.

I tapped his Ironman watch. "It's noon. They let us out to eat. We're going to Adam's for lunch."

"By golly it *is* noon!" Dad flapped.

By golly? Who said that anymore? Who ever said it? I wished he'd just carry on down the river trail. There were humongous sweat stains under his arms and around the collar of his shirt. Thank God for the breeze.

He was still standing there, like Hercules, gawking at us. "Aren't you going to introduce me to your friends?"

"Summer, Adam, this is my dad, Jim."

Adam's parents must have taught him about introductions, too, because he took my father's hand and pumped it pretty hard. "Pleased to meet you, sir." He sounded like a professional kid, or like Bobby Brown-Noser.

"Sir? I like this kid," Dad replied, smiling. "I like him a lot. And who might this be," he asked, turning to Summer.

"I'm Summer Wilson."

Dad bowed, like she was royalty. Summer turned sunburn red, tomato red and finally, hot pepper red; three shades in as many seconds. "You're the birthday girl, aren't you?"

"Yes." Summer glanced at me. "Ringo really surprised me with that gift. I've always wanted one. It was the best!"

Dad raised his bushy eyebrows. "You really liked it?"

"I wear it all the time," Summer revealed, "except today, of course. It's too hot."

I could see that Dad was majorly confused. He knew what I'd bought with the ten dollars. He must have been wondering...*this girl wears a teddy bear? How? Where? Why?*

"Uh...that's swell," he said, eyeing me.

"Dad, we've got to go. See you after school, okay?" I'd already started walking away, but Dad grabbed my arm and I steeled myself for more of his sappy humor.

"*Hang on, Sloopy*," he sang. Adam couldn't help laughing this time. He could afford to. I'd never seen *him* suffer parental humiliation. When would it end? Before I had time to bolt, Dad was inviting Adam and Summer over to help us with the big move on the weekend. Terrific.

"I'd love to help," Summer replied.

"Me, too!" Adam said. Did he have to be so chipper about it?

"Great! We'll see you then," Dad answered. His breathing had returned to normal, but sweat drenched his face and neck. "Bye for now!" Then he jogged away, long legs pumping toward the Circle Drive freeway. He'd cross the freeway bridge, then double back along the east side of the river, past the university, across the bridge, past Saskatoon City Hospital and home. He'd done it before. It nearly killed him, but old athletes die hard.

"Your dad's hilarious," Summer said as we carried on toward Adam's. I'd taken her hand again as soon as Dad left, even though mine was sticky with sweat.

"Nice of *him* to ask us over," Adam teased. He'd given me the gears before about not inviting him over. I'd told him I was an orphan, but he knew I was just holding off the inevitable family thing as long as possible. He didn't know why.

"Yep," I said, and before I knew it, I'd added, "that was swell."

Chapter Twelve

WHEN THE RAIN CAME

The weekend crashed on my doorstep. As a rule, we are not morning people, but at 6:30 Saturday morning we were eating Robin's donuts and waiting for the movers. They weren't professionals, just a couple of ex-cons with half-tons, that Mom, the equal opportunity employer, had hired.

Jane was hogging the chocolate donuts. That's what got me started. "You're not going to be hanging around all day, are you?" Come hail or high water, she'd have to be gone before my friends arrived. Thanks again, Dad.

"Like I'm going to let you touch my stuff!" she

snapped. Today she was sporting a red bandanna over her bristly head. The area around her nose ring was red and infected. Zero make-up, so there was nothing covering the dark moons under her eyes that proved she'd had too much fun the night before or too little sleep or both. Another late night with Sara, or maybe with Mike.

On her sixteenth birthday, Jane'd blown us over with a new tattoo—a large Celtic cross, on her shoulder—and a new boyfriend. Mike had a Harley; Mom had a headache for five days when she found out. It looked bad. Leather? Check. Tattoos? Check. Long hair? Double check. A good eighteen inches of it snarled down his back. Attitude? Well, he swung his shoulders like a tough guy but he wasn't so bad, we decided. He said hello and goodbye and held up his end of any conversation. He wasn't in a gang and Jane promised they weren't into anything illegal. While Mike lost points for being a high school dropout, he did at least have a steady job at an autobody shop. And he did always make sure that Jane wore a helmet.

"At least that's something," Dad reminded Mom, always looking for the good in everyone.

Moving day should have been a happy day. Finally, some space of my own, and a yard, where Mom and Dad would put in a garden. There was even a little patio out back. If only Dad hadn't invited Summer and Adam over. What if they saw Jane and recognized her as the freak at school? Sure her hair had grown a bit but there was something very distinctive about my sister. Mom said it was her demeanor. Dad said it was her individuality. Big words that amounted to the same thing: my sister had a kickass attitude.

I felt a Beatles song coming on, but then the ex-cons arrived and we had to help haul everything out.

By 10:00 a.m. we had the apartment cleared, our stored items picked up and every last thing we owned delivered to the new place. Mom paid the criminals, who really didn't look or act like they'd hurt a flea.

"Well, we've certainly got the weather on our side," Mom said, facing the maze of cardboard boxes on our front lawn. "At least for now."

The forecast called for afternoon showers, but the forecast was only right about half the time. What were the chances?

Mom and Dad made friends within minutes. One neighbor came over with a home-baked apple pie. I thought that kind of thing only happened in the country. Anyway, we thanked her then went inside and devoured it in about thirty seconds.

A couple of kids about three or four years old kept riding past our place on tricycles. Little kids didn't exactly thrill me, but they might earn me some babysitting cash. Then I could take Summer to movies. We could go wall climbing and play laser tag. Whoops. I guess I was thinking mainly of things I liked to do. I could maybe save up and buy her something wicked, like a new bike! She'd said hers was a hand-me-down from her cousin. Then she'd forget about that stupid leather jacket.

That's one good thing about dreaming. It's free. It also took my mind off my arms, which were aching from hauling box after box into the house. After unloading what I could of my own stuff, I had to start on Mom's books. Talk about heavy! Maybe it was because they were mostly about political crap, and like Dad sometimes said, a lot of politicians were full of it.

Inside, Mom was acting like a traffic officer. "Up the stairs, in the first bedroom to the right," she ordered. "No, don't set it there. Take it to the basement!"

At noon, Mike roared up on his Harley to take Jane for lunch. Dad zipped over to McDonalds to get burgers for the rest of us; it was turning into a fast food kind of day.

I hoped Jane and Michael would hit the highway and forget about coming back. It would mean more work for me, but I didn't care; Summer and Adam might show up any minute.

I was sitting on the steps swallowing the last of my Big Mac when I felt the first drops of rain. "Oh terrific!" Mom actually pulled her own hair. Even Dad scowled at the gray clouds building overhead.

Looking back, I think that the rain was the start of my bad luck. First Summer and Adam arrived. Mom spent about ten minutes interrogating them before I finally tore them away.

"Sorry," I apologized to Summer. "She's super nosy."

"No problem," Summer said. "She's just interested."

Dad was already showing Adam where to set the Boston fern when I heard the growl of a Harley at the end of the block.

I tried to lure Summer inside to help with Mom's bookshelf. "Hurry, you're getting soaked," I said, but she heard the motorcycle and waited.

They parked on the lawn. Jane unwrapped her arms from Mike's waist and kissed him, shamelessly, before he roared down the rain-slick street back to work. Adam had come out for another box. They were getting mushy with the rain. He eyed the newcomer, then edged over to where Summer stood rooted to the sidewalk.

"Hey, Ringo," Jane said, sauntering toward us.

Keep the helmet on. I was trying to will her to obey me. *Please, please, please don't let them recognize you.*

My sister crossed the grass, unsnapping her chin strap. The helmet came off with one swift movement, and so did her bandanna. A sound escaped Summer, like something being deflated.

"I'm Rox, er, Jane," Jane announced. "Ringo's sister. And you would be?"

"Summer," Summer answered. "I'm in Ringo's class."

"You're also in his underwear drawer," Jane blurted, "or at least your picture is!"

I could have killed her! Snooping in my drawer and then telling my girlfriend! Adam snickered, and Jane turned to him.

"I'm Adam," he chirped, wearing that goofy grin that showed off his chipped tooth. "I didn't know Ringo had a sister!"

Jane scratched her wet, prickly head. "What? Ringo hasn't told you about his big sister? Shame on you, Ringo." Then Jane turned her heels on the wet grass and walked inside—helmet, bandanna, ripped jeans, Harley muscle-shirt, tattoo and all.

I was hoping against everything I held sacred that Summer'd let this go. She'd never asked if I had any brothers or sisters, so at least I hadn't lied about that.

She looked like she'd seen a ghost. "You lied to me!"

I stepped back, stunned.

"You said you didn't know Jane when she came to the school. You lied to all of us!"

So much for hoping. She braced her hands on her hips and tilted her head. There was fire in her eyes.

Her accusation deserved an answer. "I, I, I—" I looked at my shoes.

"I can tolerate just about anything except a liar," Summer cried, gulping air with her words. The rain had turned her golden hair into a damp mop. "You

114

know Dad lied to me and Mom and that's why they split up. My family's a mess, and now we're a mess, too! I hate you!"

Something was tumbling inside my gut.

Breathe two three four. Breathe two three four. Tell her everything, Ringo. You must get the whole truth out.

Adam, like me, seemed too uncomfortable to move. Fortunately, Mom and Dad were busy inside. I didn't know who this girl was, although I'd had a glimpse of her once before. The girl who wrote angry poetry. I was afraid of her.

"Well?"

"Well I, I…" Damn! Why couldn't I get the words out? All I had to say was that I was so surprised to see Jane I didn't recognize her at first. She'd been living in Vancouver for several months. I'd forgotten…. Would Summer believe that crap? Not likely.

Maybe if I confessed that I was embarrassed. I mean what did everyone expect? That I'd say, "Hey, see that Neo-Nazi-looking chick out there? That's my loving sister, Jane. You should really meet her. She's been picked up for shoplifting and burnt down a house. Nice girl, though." I don't think so.

"You don't even have anything to say for yourself?"

She was giving me a second chance; I didn't take it.

"I'm outta here. Tell your parents it was nice meeting them. And don't forget Jane—*that* was special!" Summer took off, running.

There was only one good thing about the rain that day. Adam couldn't tell I was crying.

Chapter Thirteen

WITNESS

Vampires. That's what it was when I was a kid. They were forever chasing me through my dreams and waking me in the dead of night. Now it was something else. After a frightful night of running from nameless demons, I finally kicked myself free from their strangling grip and woke up.

My sheets were twisted around my ankles. I pulled myself up onto my elbows, craning my neck to see out my window into the backyard. Unbelievable. It was the middle of April and new snow covered everything, including my bike, which I'd locked to the fence. I fell back against my pillow, dreading what the day might hold.

The phone rang, but I did not jump out of bed to answer it before Mom. Moments later, she came crashing down the hall, shouting, "Get up! Get up! We slept in!"

Well isn't that just typical, I thought, lugging my legs out of bed. Today of all days, when I had to face Summer and try to explain, we slept in. Call it fate. Destiny. Blame it on that guy Murphy and his stupid law.

The family went into overdrive, scrambling to get dressed and out the door in record time. Jane actually had the advantage here. She still didn't have to do her hair, short as it was, so she was the first to leave. Mom flew out of the house with her skirt tucked into her pantyhose. Dad noticed just in time.

"I'm never gonna make my interview," he whined, grabbing a slice of burnt toast with one hand and struggling to button his shirt with the other.

"Have you seen my homework?" I asked. We hadn't finished unpacking. The house looked like a tornado had ripped through it.

Dad was fumbling with his tie. Thirty-seven years old and he still hadn't learned to knot it properly. "Mom stuck it in the laundry hamper," he said, "so it wouldn't get lost. Do I look okay?" He had his shirt buttoned up wrong, and his cowlick was rolled over to one side like a wave.

"Very professional," I lied. I found my books under a pile of dirty clothes, then ducked into the bathroom to slap water on my crown.

118

Dad was on my heels. He jostled me away from the mirror and faced his reflection. "Oh no! Bed head!" he cried. I was already halfway down the hall.

It was 9:01 when I jumped off the steps of the house. The world was bleak. It could have been November. I wondered if the wild weather had anything to do with how we kept screwing up the earth's atmosphere. Mom said gas fumes and something called PCB's were causing big holes in the ozone layer and letting in some bad rays. It sounded like the kind of thing she could get really passionate about. I imagined her parading back and forth in front of city hall, wearing a sandwich board that said: STYROFOAM KILLS or LOVE THIS PLANET? THEN GET ON THE BALL…JUST SAY NO TO AEROSOL.

My feet were getting wet in my shoes as I scuffed them down the avenue. I hated being late. It was almost as bad as walking into class on the first day. Everyone stopped what they were doing and looked at you suspiciously, and no excuse would be good enough for Ms. Harmon, considering the mood she'd been in lately.

I started to run. My feet seemed to be slapping out a chant as they hit the snow-covered pavement. West Park. West Park. West Park. West Park.

I was about to cut through the school parking lot when I saw a figure crouch between Ms. Harmon's Honda and a silver Saturn. Everyone should have been inside. I hid behind the garbage disposal bin.

A head popped up, covered in a black toque. I tiptoed closer, hiding behind a minivan. Then the figure stood. I knew that red and black checked lumber jacket, those wide shoulders and legs like tree trunks. Larry! He spun around as if he could hear his name in my thoughts. I ducked behind the minivan, my heart a grenade ready to blow. I waited, then, hoping the coast was clear, peeked to see Larry leaving the parking lot for the school. When I was sure he was well inside, I ran over to inspect the cars. Ms. Harmon's tires had been slashed!

"You're late." It was Mr. Crawford, not Ms. Harmon at the front of our room. A mustached police officer in full uniform was looking very official beside our vice-principal. "First Larry, and now you," Mr. Crawford continued. "Glad you've decided to join us. Now come in and close the door."

I slid into my desk, wishing once again that the floor would open up and swallow me.

"We're here to talk to you about some very disturbing things that have been happening, things you may not be aware of," Mr. Crawford began. "They concern Ms. Harmon."

There were several murmurs in the classroom. I turned to Summer out of instinct and hoped that she would also turn to look at me, but she didn't.

"Your teacher has been under considerable stress for some time now, and for good reason. There have been obscene phone calls in the middle of the night, eggs thrown at her windows and garbage strewn across her yard. Last Thursday night, while she was here at a staff meeting, her home was broken into and vandalized."

His words were streaks with long tails of fire. I remembered Summer telling me about the day she'd found Ms. Harmon crying. It must have had something to do with this. The cop took a notepad out of his pocket, flipped it open and began reading. "At approximately 10:15 p.m.Thursday, Ms. Harmon returned to her home to find the back door had been pried open. Inside, walls had been spray painted with obscene words, furniture was slashed, food and other matter were smeared into rugs and walls. Damages are estimated at around seven thousand dollars."

Other matter? I instinctively plugged my nose.

Mr. Crawford had been pacing up and down between the aisles. He stopped to sit on the edge of Ms. Harmon's desk. "Now we're not suggesting that anyone here had anything to do with this," he said, "but we must explore all possibilities." He drummed his long fingers against the top of the desk. "What may have begun as relatively harmless pranks have now become serious crimes. Officer Rogers here is going to be interviewing each of you in my office. I expect your full co-operation."

Breathe two three four. Breathe two three four. Breath

two three four. Breathe two three four.

We were following the seating order for the interviews. Larry'd been gone for what seemed like a lifetime. The door finally swung open and the monster came back in. He gave me the finger when Mr. Crawford wasn't looking.

"Ringo...your turn."

My feet were two ice blocks that I had to drag to the office. There was a skin of suspense over everything.

"Go ahead," the secretary said, nodding toward the open door, "they're waiting for you."

They're waiting? I forced my feet forward and was shocked to see Ms. Harmon in a chair next to the police officer. There were dark rings under her eyes, as though she hadn't slept since September.

"Hello, Ringo," she said, her voice coming out soft in the dark-walled room. Then, to the police officer, "This is the young man I told you about."

What? They'd been talking about me? I wondered how in the world Larry had done it. How had he managed to pin this crime on me. Was he the devil himself?

"I understand that you've had some trouble with a certain classmate," the officer began. "Would you care to tell me about that?"

I don't know how I got through the next several minutes, but I managed to bumble through some of

Larry's misdemeanors against me.

"Ringo, I don't want you to take this the wrong way," Ms. Harmon said, "but the harassment seemed to start shortly after you arrived at West Park. I don't believe you would do anything to harm me or anyone else, but if you know anything about these events, this is the time to speak up."

Seconds passed.

"Have you seen or heard anything that might be connected to this investigation?" the officer asked.

A long, bony finger of fright ran up the length of my spine and I shivered. Ms. Harmon was waiting. The cop was waiting. Waiting to pump me for info. I knew that sitting in that classroom, third aisle in, second desk from the front, Larry was waiting, too. Then, out of some distant corner of my mind, I heard the echo of two distinct voices: *You lied to me. You lied to all of us. I can tolerate anything but a liar.*

An accident! What's wrong with you?

The voices began to overlap, like waves against a shore. *Lied to us...accident...anything but...what's wrong?*

I was drowning. I had to make them stop. "This morning. I, I saw Larry. He, he—"

"Go on, Ringo," Ms. Harmon prompted. She leaned over and put her hand on my quivering shoulder.

"He slashed your tires."

Chapter Fourteen

STARTING OVER

They found the switchblade inside his boot, and not a moment too soon. We'd *both* been late for class that day. If it weren't for Ms. Harmon's faith in me, I could have been suspected of the slashing.

We were told that Larry'd be questioned further about both the harassments and the vandalism. Apparently, after I'd stepped forward, Bobby B., Matt, Jesse, Logan and Shawn also linked Larry to a number of crimes. Idiot that he was, he'd bragged about tormenting Ms. Harmon. She said she suspected all along that Larry was the one secretly harassing her. She didn't go into too much detail, but she did tell us that he'd been neglected much of his life and acting out was the only way he knew how to get attention. For Larry, even negative attention was better than nothing at all. He was getting professional help now, but we wouldn't see him back at West Park ever again, and that was good enough for me.

No one else had planned to utter a word about Larry until I ratted. No one else had the guts. No one else was that crazy.

The word spread like cancer through the entire school: Ringo Warren was the first to rat. After the final bell, I trudged down the Trans-Canada hall, my backpack three times heavier than usual, though I wasn't carrying anything at all. I could actually feel people talking about me. Their words were little rocks that pinged against my neck and arms. *Just let this miserable day end*, I thought.

"Ringo?"

I turned to the voice I knew so well. "You...you're talking to me?" I pinched my arm. I wasn't dreaming.

"I'm proud of you," Summer said, "what you did today took a lot of nerve."

You could have knocked me over with a feather.

"I'm still upset that you lied about Jane, but I'm going to give you another chance. It's just that...my dad—"

"I know," I said, putting my finger to her lips. "He lied, too."

"Uh huh."

I felt half the tense muscles in my shoulders and back relax.

"Summer?" It was on the tip of my tongue. I could almost taste the words. I was finally going to come clean. "At your party, there was something I really needed to—"

"Hey you guys!" Tori yelled, running up between us. "School's over. Let's get out of here!"

Not again!

"Ringo!" Adam called. "We've got a date with our bikes, remember?"

"I'll be right with you, Bud," I said, recalling the plan to cycle around the river.

I squeezed Summer's hand. "Can I call you tonight?"

"Of course," she said. "What were you going to say about the party?" Her green eyes were mesmerizing, her hand so soft in mine. With just a few words I could shatter everything.

"I forget," I said. "Maybe it'll come to me later."

Chapter Fifteen

SHOWDOWN

Mom and Dad were celebrating. "It's a great job," Mom squealed, for about the fiftieth time since they'd got the good news. "Monday to Friday, union, full benefits, decent starting wage."

"Plus, it's just across the river!" Dad spurted. "I can run to work!"

The man was beaming like a lighthouse. He was starting his full-time job in maintenance at Royal University Hospital on Tuesday, right after the May long weekend.

"Now remember, we're at Martini's." Dad helped Mom into her beige trench coat. "The number's beside the phone, and Jane should be home early."

"Yeah, yeah," I whined. "Cripes, I'm not a baby."

"You'll always be our baby," Mom gushed. She squeezed my shoulders.

"Get outta here and have some fun," I ordered, shooing them out. "And don't do anything I wouldn't do!"

I watched them back out of the driveway, then checked my watch. Seven bells. Summer, Adam and Tori would be arriving soon. We'd planned a long weekend celebration of our own, and there was much to celebrate. For one, Larry was long gone from West Park and I felt like an elephant had been lifted from my shoulders. I could breathe.

Adam and Tori had started going out, another reason to celebrate. The four of us had cycled around the Meewasin Trail, gone glow bowling and seen a few movies together. Mostly we just hung out at the Midtown Plaza or the Mall at Lawson Heights. Life was almost perfect.

I swept off the patio and arranged the chairs around the table. We'd play cards, listen to music and drink fruity drinks in tall glasses with sliced pineapples stuck on the rims. I didn't expect my parents back early, but I'd told them my friends might stop over, just in case. Jane was out with Mike, and had said she wouldn't be home early. "So don't hold your breath waiting for me," she advised, behind Mom and Dad's back. "I wouldn't want you to croak."

Wisecracks aside, Jane was a new person. Maybe it was because she was dating an older guy. Despite his tough appearance, Mike was more mature than all the other guys Jane had gone out with put together, and that added up to a lot. I guess it's true what they say— you can't judge a book by its cover. Even Mom was warming to him. She was able to look past the grease-stained hands and the snake tattooed on his forearm.

Jane resembled a human being again. Her hair was long enough to comb, and sometimes when she dressed up a bit I saw what Adam saw, and what Jeff in Gibsons told me he'd seen…my sister was actually not bad looking. At least she wouldn't break any mirrors.

"She's made great strides," Mom'd said, earlier that day. I'd pressed my ear to the hot air register in the bathroom, which was like a direct line into the family room where Mom and Dad were talking. "You know what she said to me the other day? She said she felt like she finally belonged in this family." I quickly pulled away from my listening post. I didn't want to know too much, in case I jinxed the umbrella of calm we were living under.

I checked the yard one more time. Everything was in place except a pile of bricks that had been dumped near the house. Dad was making a winding brick path to the garage. I straightened the bricks and was just slapping the dust off my hands when the gate creaked open.

"Hey, Ringo!" My friends were three splashes of color against the white fence. We'd decided to wear our brightest summer clothes to welcome the warm weather.

Adam's knobby knees stuck out from underneath long red and orange shorts. His eyes were hidden behind dark shades. Blues and greens swirled together on a tie-dyed shirt that was so tight it pulled his shoulders forward. "I made it at summer camp," he explained, "four years ago."

Summer set a Macs bag on the table and—my heart sunk to the middle of my belly—draped her leather jacket over the back of a chair. "Ta-da" she sang, twirling her long, floral dress like a Spanish dancer. Black leather sandals laced up her slender ankles. Her hair was loose over her shoulders, and I realized how much it'd grown over the winter. "I brought the jacket in case it cools off later."

"G-good idea," I mumbled.

"I've got chips and nachos," Tori said, dropping the munchies on the table. She was in shorts and a crop-top with a sunflower design. Her brown curls poked out from beneath a straw hat with a cloth sunflower pinned to the front. "Nice outfit," she said, eyeing the purple and yellow number I'd pulled together for the evening. She clapped her hands over her ears. "Very loud."

I invited my friends to have a seat at the patio table while I poured our tropical drinks and brought them out. I'd set a blaster near the back door. After much searching, I managed to find something other than my parents' Beatles tracks and Jane's headbanger music. I clicked the machine on as I passed.

"What's this?" Adam asked when the music reached his ears.

"Don't you know?" Summer bounced to the happy beat. "This is Bob Marley. Reggae. It's summer music. A perfect way to ring in the new season."

My girlfriend was constantly surprising me. She knew about so many things: music, Hitchcock movies, filleting fish, how to change a bike tire or deal with a bleeding wound. She even knew about Shakespeare. She said that they have something here called *Shakespeare on the Saskatchewan*. "They hold plays under a big tent on the riverbank. You should come, Ringo."

I told her I would.

Adam showed us a card trick. He tried to shuffle like a pro, but the cards flipped out of his hands and flew into the air.

"You rock, Adam!" I teased.

"They're like wings!" Summer said, laughing as the cards hit the ground.

She had a way of seeing things like no one else, just as I had a talent for hearing what others didn't. Sometimes the rustle of last year's leaves in the grass was almost deafening. Or I'd be sitting in my desk at school and I'd hear someone four rows over, breathing. It freaked me out!

That night, all my senses were super keen. The smell from a barbecue down the block made my mouth water and I could almost taste the juicy steak, smothered in tangy sauce. My thoughts jumped from one sound or smell or image to another, like jump cuts in a rock video. From the dark sky and the first few pinpoints of starry light to Summer's hand on my arm. From the flat face of the King of Hearts to the bongo drums in Marley's music. The sun settled behind our house and then the moon somersaulted across the sky. Everything was in its proper place, but just this once I wanted to stop the world from spinning. I wanted the night to last forever.

Then, another sound, a snap from the trees at the back of the yard. "Did you guys hear something?" I turned, listening for another snap from the darkness. It came.

Summer and I locked eyes. Adam raised his hand—a signal for everyone to be still. I reached behind me and killed the music.

We heard it again. Like the snapping of brittle bone. "Who's there?"

Adam and I leapt up like white knights ready to slay the dragon and defend our damsels. We heard a moan, like an animal dying a slow death. The white knights took a baby step forward.

Then the sound became human. First, the mocking, singsong voice. "There was a farmer had a dog...and Ringo was his name-o."

Larry flew out of the trees and fell onto the grass.

"Larry!" Adam shouted.

Tori shrieked. "What are you doing here?"

The moonlight was playing tricks. Larry's shadow stretched and swallowed us as he slowly and steadily approached. A meter away, I could smell what he'd been drinking. He pulled a slim bottle out of his jean jacket and belted back the dark liquid.

"Hello boys and girls." A single twig was tangled in his long hair. He belched, took another sip, then asked: "Are we having fun yet?"

Strength in numbers, Ringo. When the going gets tough the tough get going. Names will never hurt you.

All those clichés that are supposed to bring comfort brought little to me then. If the girls hadn't been there I might have run into the house and locked the door, but I don't think so. After taking Larry's abuse for so many months, I was finally ready to act.

"Take a hike, Larry."

He didn't budge. I pushed him in the chest and he stumbled back.

"Ringo!" Summer cried.

Larry lurched forward, fists ready to fly, but I stood

my ground. Adam slipped between us, arms out, like a referee.

"Take it easy, guys. We can talk this out."

"There's nothing to talk about!" I snapped, over Adam's shoulder into Larry's face. We were almost eyeball to eyeball, with Adam sandwiched between us. "What in the hell is wrong with you? You're evil. You hurt people. You tormented Ms. Harmon. You're a loser, Larry, a serious scumbag."

"Ringo!" Summer was pulling at my arm, but like the water at the weir, the words kept rolling.

"There's no hope for you. Once a loser, always a loser."

Surprisingly, Larry didn't kill me right then and there. He didn't use sticks and stones. First he laughed, like my words meant nothing. I suppose he's heard much worse. Then: "Have you told her yet?"

Summer stepped forward. "Told who what?"

"So you haven't," Larry said. He took another swig. "She *still* doesn't know."

"Ringo. What's he talking about?"

Larry threw his head back and howled at the moon. It was what he'd been waiting for: the moment of truth. He'd been saving it for exactly the right time and that time had arrived. I was squirming.

"The jacket," Larry said. "Your precious leather jacket."

Summer was hanging on to me now. "What about

134

my jacket?"

"I'm glad you liked it," Larry answered, before I could spit out a single word. "Sure beat the hell out of that teddy bear, didn't it?" He laughed, but the sound had a razor edge to it. "*I* bought the jacket. Ringo here bought the bear."

Summer glanced from Larry to me. "Ringo, what's he...?"

"I'm so, so sorry," I began, taking her gently by the wrists. "Larry switched our gifts at your party and before I could say anything you were trying on that leather jacket and thanking me for it and everyone was going on and on about it and I just couldn't," I stumbled, feeling her tear away from me, "I just...just couldn't tell you that all I'd really bought you was that cheap little teddy bear."

There were tears, not of rage, but of something else in Summer's eyes. The lights were gone. "I don't care about the damn jacket, or the teddy bear! Don't you know that? I care that you promised not to lie and here you've been keeping this from me all along. I thought we were friends, Ringo. Confidants. Doesn't that mean anything to you? I thought I could trust you. How could you keep this from me?" Her voice broke. "H-How? I told everyone what you gave me, or what I *thought* you gave me. I bragged you up all over town."

"Summer, I wanted to tell you," I said, "but each time I tried we'd either get interrupted or I'd lose my nerve."

"It's true—" Adam tried, but Tori cut him off.

"*You* stay out of this!" she yelled. "You probably knew all along, didn't you?"

Adam dragged his hand through his hair. "W-well..."

"Listen, I'm very, very sorry," I pleaded, forgetting about our audience. Right then, it was me and Summer, alone in the universe. "Things just got outta hand."

Summer swiped tears from her cheek. "You're sorry? Well, I'm sorry, too, Ringo." Her shoulders were shaking, big time. I dreaded what was coming next.

"It's over," she said. "This time, it's really over." She backed away, giving me the full benefit of the pain in her wet eyes, her drooping arms, the shoulders that folded in. Her entire body was a rack of despair. She stopped where she'd draped the jacket over her chair. "You'll have to find someone else to lie to from now on." She heaved the jacket at me. It fell to the grass like a dead animal.

"We're gone," Tori sniped, looping her arm through Summer's in solidarity.

"Wait!" I tried, but it was already too late. The curtain had fallen, and the girls fled through the gate into the night.

Adam was shaking his head. "Great," he mumbled, "that's just great."

"Encore!" Larry heckled. He doubled in wild laughter. "Wanna drown your sorrows?" He held out his bottle and the murky contents swished inside.

I slapped his arm away. "You son of a..."

He drained his bottle on the grass, then smashed it on the patio, sending shards flying across the cement and grass.

"Whoops!" He headed for the gate. "Sorry to leave so soon, but someone owes me for a gift, and believe me, I'm going to collect."

That was it! I charged Larry, elbows out, and knocked him over. Then he grabbed my ankle and the ground zoomed up to meet me. SLAM!

"Ringo!" Adam yelled. He tried pulling me to my feet but I'd had the wind knocked out of me and wasn't sure whether I was up or down.

"Adam, behind you!" I yelled. Too late. Larry'd grabbed Adam around the waist, tearing him away from me. He flung Adam around like a puppet, then let go. Adam veered toward the house, but Larry was too fast. He karate-kicked Adam in the back, and the last thing I heard before my friend hit the cement was one sorry vowel: ohhhh.

It wasn't over. As Adam lay still, I watched, helpless, while Larry gave him two swift kicks in the ribs. Blood oozed from Adam's head.

Get up, Ringo! Move!

I sucked the pain in, rose and plunged toward them. I grabbed Larry's jacket, wrenching him away.

"You're dead," he hissed, spinning on me. My fist

cracked against his temple, his jutting chin. He got me with an uppercut to the jaw. So big, I thought. So much power. I crumpled with a fierce blow to my stomach, gulping down deep breaths so I wouldn't pass out.

I fought with everything I had, but he kept coming back with his bigger fists, his stronger arms, with feet and knees that were everywhere all at once. I tasted blood.

"Adam!" I called, dodging a blow, but my friend was curled onto his side, motionless, silent.

My head was a beehive full of stings. All my nerves and muscles screamed. Then Larry bulldozed me again and we fell onto the grass.

Something jabbed. The broken bottle! I was lying on shattered glass! Larry was clawing the grass like an animal. He rolled onto me, pinning my arms and several small shards of glass beneath me. Then he showed me his prize—one sharp triangle.

"Why?" I wheezed, my chest pounding as he straddled me with all his weight. I struggled to focus on his face.

"'Cause I've been watching you since day one," Larry hissed. "Saw you with your parents...hanging out with your buds. What's that like? To have people care whether you live or die? My parents say I was an accident. They'd lock me in my room. Pretend I didn't exist. Now they buy me off. NOBODY WANTS ME!"

Larry was sobbing, his face a blur.

"Then Summer's party. The new kid's in with the hottest girls. And there's me…on the outside looking in. Again. IT'S NOT FAIR!"

He shook my shoulders, the glass near my ear.

"Betcha can't guess how many birthday parties I've had?"

I spit up blood.

"One. One freakin' party and I was so excited, I didn't even know how to act. I was six-years-old, and I blew it. I never had anyone over again!"

I was fading. Fast. I thought I heard a distant, rumbling sound, like a tornado approaching, or maybe it was the river, roaring through my veins. I didn't know what was real anymore.

"The way Ms. Harmon smiled at you…dates with the golden girl… yeah, I know all about your life, Ringo. Your short life."

Larry raised the glass and I pinched my eyes shut. "NNNNOOOOO!"

"RINGO!"

There was a sickening thud. I felt my chest inflate as Larry slid off me, unconscious. I opened one swollen eye and saw my sister, the red brick still in her hand.

Chapter Sixteen

THE LAST THING TO HEAL

Adam had two broken ribs and a concussion. I had bruises everywhere, and, after they'd removed the shards of glass from my back and legs, twelve stitches. But we survived.

Larry was also going to live, but he wouldn't be hurting anyone else for a long, long time. Ironically, now it was up to the courts to figure out what to do with him, and this time, I don't think his parents would have any say at all.

Larry said he knew everything about me, but he'd missed one thing: I have a sister. She may have a kickass attitude but I'm her brother and she loves me. I believe she saved my life.

Mom offered to stay home with me while I took a few days off school to heal. I said she didn't have to, but I think the story about Larry's neglect hit a nerve with her. She's been spending a lot more time with me and Jane.

Ms. Harmon came by with cards from my classmates while I was healing at home. She said she was sorry for not recognizing how serious Larry's problems were, and I thought she was going to start bawling. Summer's tears had been more than enough already. I told my teacher not to worry, it was over now. Besides, she had her own healing to do.

After she left I began to pick through the pile of different cards. Heather decorated hers with colorful flowers. Christy threaded a ribbon through hers. Amanda's was shaped like a heart. Jesse and Johnathon had scribbled on sheets torn from their notebooks, and Logan signed his message on an origami swan. Instead of signing his name, Matt sent a picture of himself. Bobby B. wanted to know if there was "anything at all" he could do to help speed my recovery. It was good to see that some things hadn't changed.

It seemed only fitting that the Beatles' tune *A Little Help From My Friends* should be playing while I read the get well cards, but this time it wasn't in my head. Larry'd knocked the music out. Mom had it on the CD.

I came to Summer's note. It was typed on plain white

paper and folded into thirds like a formal business letter.

> Ringo:
> I was very sorry to hear about what
> happened. I hope you're feeling better
> soon.
>
> *Summer Wilson*

And that was it. As cold and impersonal as the company rejection letters my dad used to get.

You've had it all wrong, Ringo. You realize that now, don't you?

Yes, I did realize it then. All those months I was terrified about what Larry might do to me. I worried about getting my teeth chipped or my bones knocked around, but that wasn't what was important at all. Now I believe that a person can get over almost any kind of physical pain, but the last thing to heal is the heart.

Epilogue

It's July. I am biking along the river trail, alone. The muscles in my thirteen-year-old legs are tight as wires and although it tries the wind can't slow me down. I am riding planet earth. I am flying.

I reach an area where water flows between large rocks. I set the crossbar of my bike on one shoulder and carefully step over the rocks, glad for my strength. On the other side, the trail narrows to a dirt path barely wide enough for my tires.

As many times as I've ridden this route over the last few months, I never really know what's next. The trees seem to change; grass grows. Beavers do their damage, and sometimes there are broken beer bottles or the sad-looking remains of campfires that weren't there just days before. Much has happened and I need this time alone to process it. I get glimpses of *understanding* when the wind's singing through my hair and branches are smacking me in the face. I understand why Larry felt he had to do what he did. He was just living up to everyone's expectations of him, and if it wouldn't have been me, it would have been someone else. I understand why Summer felt she couldn't see me again, based on her father's history of lies. I think I'm even beginning to understand that my life will go on, with or without Summer in it. I still have Adam, and that's something.

The long arms of branches spread across my path. I miss some and take others full in the face. Night is falling all around me. My lungs pound. My mouth is so dry I taste blood, but it's good to be free from everything, to think of nothing except my muscles working together like a team.

I stand on my pedals to climb a steep hill, then wing it on the way down, hair flying into my eyes. A rock springs up out of nowhere and my handlebars jack-knife. I'm thrown into the prickly grass between two clumps of trees. And then I dream of a girl, shimmering in the moonlight. She takes my hand and leads me to the river where we cling to each other, inches from the water on the flat back of a rock.

"Do you hear it?" I ask.

She leans back against my chest.

Everything's playing in my head at once. Acoustic guitars and bongo drums. Dad's telling John Lennon about the marathon he's training for; Mom's having tea with Ringo Starr. There's a crowd running with bulls down the streets of a country I do not know. My inner voice says *Jolly good, Ringo—jolly good.* Jane's yelling, "Catch 'ya later!" as she roars off on Mike's Harley. I hear stars sigh, the moon pull and the current of my own blood, rushing.

Life has made a poet out of me.

I ask my companion again. "Do you hear it?"

She listens. "I think so. What is it?"

Whatever I answer, it will be true.

Shelley A. Leedahl writes books for people of all ages. Like Ringo's father, she loves running along the river, and like Ringo, she loves to hear the wind singing through her hair.

Shelley lives with Troy, Logan and Taylor in Saskatoon.

Photo credit: Troy Leedahl